Pony Club Cup

KU-176-450

About the author

Josephine Pullein-Thompson was brought up in the country. Her mother strongly disapproved of schools, but approved of books and ponies. Especially ponies, which she said were safer than bicycles.

At the age of eleven, Josephine broke in her first pony. When she was fifteen she gave up her occasional visits to school and with her sisters, twins Diana and Christine, began to teach riding. They eventually opened their own riding school and also became whippers-in to the Woodland Foxhounds. They also started to write stories. Their first pony book, a joint effort, was published when they were in their teens. Josephine has since written over thirty books: pony stories, books on riding and training horses, and a few murders for adults. Her most popular children's books were about the West Barsetshire Pony Club, first published in the 1940s. She has been connected with the Pony Club all her life and for many years was the District Commissioner of the Woodland Pony Club in Oxfordshire.

Pony Club Cup is the first book in the series about the Woodbury Pony Club. The second and third books, *Pony Club Challenge* and *Pony Club Trek*, are also available in Armada.

Josephine Pullein-Thompson

Pony Club Cup

An Armada Original

Pony Club Cup was first published
in the U.K. in Armada in 1983
by Fontana Paperbacks,
8 Grafton Street, London W1X 3LA

Armada is an imprint of Fontana Paperbacks,
part of the Collins Publishing Group

This impression 1986

Printed in Great Britain by
William Collins Sons & Co. Ltd, Glasgow

Contents

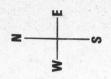

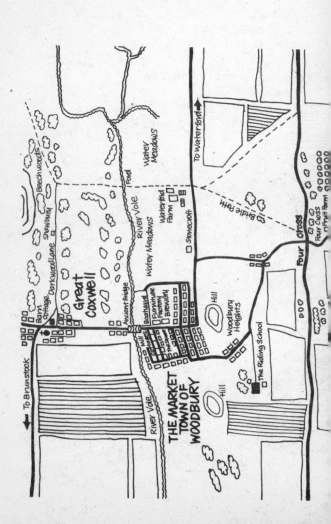

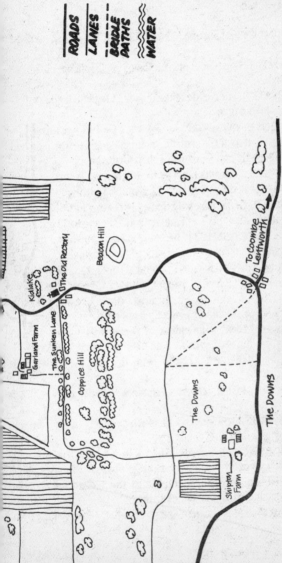

ROADS
LANES
BRIDLE PATHS
WATER

Kidlake
The Old Rectory
Beacon Hill
Garland Farm
The Sunken Lane
Coppice Hill
The Downs
Skipton Farm
The Downs
To Coombe
Lentworth

MAP OF WOODBURY & DISTRICT

Members and Officials of the Woodbury Branch of the Pony Club

DAVID LUMLEY, ex steeple-chase jockey. Lives at Garland Farm.

MRS. ROOKE, Hon. Secretary. Lives at 20, The Heights, Woodbury.

LESLEY ROOKE, her eldest daughter. Owns Stardust, 14-hands chestnut mare.

SARAH ROOKE owns Chess, 13-hands piebald gelding.

MR. & MRS. ROBERTS run Garland Farm for David Lumley. They live at Garland Farm Cottage.

LYNNE ROBERTS owns Berry, 13.1 red roan mare.

PAUL ROBERTS owns Banjo, 12.2 black gelding.

ALICE DRUMMOND hires Saffron, 14.1 dun gelding. Lives with her uncle and aunt at Shawbury, Darkwood Lane.

MARGARET & PETER HUTCHINSON, Alice's aunt and uncle.

CLARE HUTCHINSON, one of Alice's four cousins.

HANIF (HARRY) FRANKLIN owns Jupiter, 14.2 liver chestnut gelding. Lives at Barn Cottage, Great Coxwell.

JAMES MORGAN shares Ferdinand, dark brown gelding, with his mother. Lives at Four Cross Fruit Farm.

RUPERT WHEELER, the eldest of the family, owns Rosie, 14.1 light bay mare. Lives at The Old Rectory, Kidlake.

ELIZABETH WHEELER owns Rajah, 14.1½ chestnut gelding.

ANNETTE WHEELER owns Tristram, 13.2 grey Welsh gelding.

OLIVER WHEELER owns Hobbit, 12.2 dark brown Dartmoor gelding.

JENNIFER BLACKER owns Sea King, 14.2 bright bay gelding. Lives at Stonecroft on the Waterford Road.

TINA SPENCER. No pony. Helps at the riding school and lives at 5 Mill Cottages, Woodbury.

JULIA CARTWRIGHT and JANET GREEN. Pony Club instructors.

CHAPTER ONE

"What's He Like?"

"I shouldn't think it *could* get worse. I mean fewer and fewer people are turning up, and you can't blame them when the instruction's so useless," said James Morgan gloomily, as he rode dark brown Ferdinand along the lane, walking stride for stride with Jennifer Blacker's Sea King. "Rallies weren't much fun when Mrs Smythe was D.C., but at least you learned a bit."

"Yes, and she always got really good people to instruct the top ride, but now we're in the top ride we still have Janet or Julia or Mr Foster's working pupils taking us. And those working pupils are *pathetic*, all theory. They don't ride as well as we do," complained Jennifer in a voice of deep disgust.

"We're only in the top ride because all the older members have stopped coming," James pointed out. "I do hope this new bloke fizzes things up a bit."

"But I don't see how an ex-jockey for D.C. *can* improve things. They only know how to ride in races."

"He's an ex-*jump* jockey, so with any luck he'll have us belting over steeplechase fences," said James, his solid face brightening.

"Well I'm not going to risk spoiling King just as he's begun to win," Jennifer spoke decidedly, as she patted her pony's bright bay neck. "I'm going to have another go at Mummy about transferring to the Cranford Vale. They're a decent pony club, much the best round here. They had a team in practically all the finals last year. The trouble is that their rallies are such miles away. It's too far to hack and Mummy says that with petrol the price it is, she can't afford to use the trailer for rallies as well as shows."

"Hadn't you better hang on for a bit and see if things improve?" suggested James.

"No, I'm not going to bother with it any more. If Mummy won't let me transfer I'll just give up the pony club," said Jennifer, her pale, flat face set in obstinate lines. "How can a smashed-up jockey know anything about proper riding."

"David Lumley knows a lot."

James and Jennifer turned in their saddles to see Paul Roberts jogging along behind them on his little black pony, Banjo. Paul was small for his age, which was eleven, had a small neat face which matched the rest of him, and serious grey eyes. He had listened to their conversation and now forced himself to speak up.

"David was in the pony club when he was young. He did a lot of ordinary riding and then he took to breaking and schooling and riding in horse trials *before* he became a national hunt jockey. He was top class, and all set to be Champion Jockey when he had his smash."

"You know this Lumley bloke?" asked James in surprise.

"Yes, you see my sister Lynne and I live at Garland Farm. Well, David Lumley lives in the farmhouse and we live in the cottages and my father runs the farm for him," explained Paul, wishing that Lynne, who was a year older, would stop giggling with Netti Wheeler and Sarah Rooke and help him stand up for David.

"All the rallies are going to be held over at our place, at Garland Farm, in future," he told them.

"Yes, we know that, Mrs Rooke announced it. But what's he *like*?"

"My mother knows all about him," Lesley Rooke, who'd been riding alone as usual—no one really liked her—pulled up when she heard James's question. "He wasn't all that keen to be D.C.," she went on, the sun glinting on her thick-lensed glasses as she kicked her pretty chestnut pony, Stardust, closer to the group. "Someone on the pony club committe heard that Mr Lumley had shut himself up and was moping, because he can't ride any more, so they decided he needed something to occupy him and talked him into it."

"He's not going to be much good if he's not really interested," said James gloomily.

"Well, there isn't anyone else. People round here won't take on thankless tasks like the pony club. My mother doesn't really want to be secretary—it's a lot of work—but no one else will do it." Lesley's wide, slightly cow-like face, with its broad nose and thick lips, looked pleased at this proof of meanness in local people.

"I think David *is* quite interested now that he's made up his mind to it," objected Paul. "He and Dad have been talking over which fields they'll use and things like that. But it's how he's going to manage, being so lame and having an arm that doesn't work at all; he can't lift a jump or buckle a bridle . . .".

"He sounds a bit of a wreck to me," grumbled James.

The four Wheelers, who had had to go back to the field where the rally was held to find Rupert's forgotten head-collar, clattered in pursuit of the other pony club members. Long-legged Rupert, the eldest of the four, was riding Rosie, a light bay mare with a mealy nose, a strong-looking pony of fourteen-two. Lizzie, who was next to Rupert in age, owned Rajah, a lean, sober, chestnut gelding, darker in colour and more solidly-built than Lesley Rooke's Stardust. You could tell that Rupert and Lizzie were brother and sister, they had the same pink and white faces, blue eyes and pale, straw-coloured hair, but Rupert's face was longer, his blue eyes dreamy, his hair short and curly. Lizzie had an anxious face, as though she expected things to go wrong, and she wore her hair in one long, thick, flaxen plait.

Behind, came the two younger Wheelers. Annette, she was always called Netti, had short curly hair like Rupert, but her face was heart-shaped and her eyes weren't dreamy or anxious, they had a sparkle which suggested that she enjoyed life and excitement and adventures. Netti was riding Tristram, a little grey Welsh pony who had been outgrown by Rupert. Beside her, Oliver, the youngest of the Wheelers, bounced about on Hobbit, a dark-brown Dartmoor who had once been Lizzie's pony.

"If he's a jockey perhaps he'll let us race instead of all this awful, boring schooling," shouted Oliver, who rode very badly but hated being taught.

"Mrs Rookery didn't really tell us anything about him," complained Rupert. "Lynne," he shouted, "wait for us, we want to know what this new guy is like."

Lynne Roberts was quite different from her younger brother Paul. She had wavy, light-brown hair which stuck out from her plump, cheerful face, and when she laughed, which was most of the time, her hazel-coloured eyes disappeared into the plumpness and became slits. She wasn't a very good rider, but she loved Berry, her red roan pony, and didn't mind that she wasn't very well-schooled and couldn't jump.

"What's he like, really, this David Lumley?" Rupert asked again as he caught up.

"He used to be very nice, always full of jokes," answered Lynne, "but the accident's changed him. Mum says it'll pass off, that it's only the pain and frustration that's making him irritable, but the doctors don't think he'll ever recover completely. They said he'd probably never ride again."

"What exactly happened to him?" asked Oliver, who enjoyed gruesome details.

"It was in some big race, not the Grand National. He's ridden in that lots of times. The Gold Cup, I think. The horse in front fell and brought his horse down and then a third one landed on top of him. It was terribly sad, two of the horses had to be shot and David was unconscious for over a week. Then, when he came round, he was partly paralysed: he couldn't walk or use his left hand, and, on top of that he had lots of broken bones."

"Poor him, how awful," said Lizzie, her voice full of concern.

"Is anyone going to the Brunstock show?" Sarah Rooke changed the subject. She was much prettier than her elder sister, Lesley, and didn't have to wear glasses. Her face was narrow and she wore her dark hair in a fringe. But it wasn't a friendly face, and her rather thin-lipped mouth gave her a determined look, as though she always got her own way.

12

Chess, her pony, was a stout little piebald of about thirteen hands.

"No shows for us these holidays," answered Lizzie. "Mummy's gone on strike over entry fees and anyway we never win anything.'

"I'm going in for the gymkhana, there are masses of events for twelve and unders. You ought to come, Netti."

"I don't really want to, not without the others. It's no fun hacking miles on your own. And with the Cranford Vale Prince Philip-ers there I wouldn't stand a chance. Even their B team is absolutely brilliant."

"The Great Sarah thinks she's good enough to beat them," sneered Lesley Rooke in a very spiteful voice, as they caught up with the group ahead.

"I didn't say anything of the sort," Sarah snapped back.

"Well, Mummy thinks you are. She's paying your entry fees."

She'd have paid yours, only she knows you haven't a hope in the under sixteen classes."

"I can't help my age . . ."

"Oh, shut up. Little Rookes in their nest should agree and not keep cawing in spiteful voices," Rupert told them.

"I do wish there was a jumping class for *small* ponies," sighed Paul. "Show-jumping is Banjo's best thing, but he can't go in Under 14.2 classes and its no fun going in Clear Round Jumping, show after show. You haven't really won the rosette and anyway I want to jump off against the clock."

"Daddy say's we're wet and that we should run our own gymkhanas and *get* as good as the Cranford Vale," Netti Wheeler told Paul. "But Rupert and Lizzie have gone off competitions now that they've got new and bigger ponies which aren't much good at anything, and Ollie and I aren't exactly brilliant at organization."

When the lane brought them to a road, the Rookes turned the opposite way to the rest of the riders, and trotted, in silent single file towards Woodbury Heights, the Victorian part of the old market town of Woodbury, where they lived in a tall, red-brick house.

13

At the next crossroads Jennifer Blacker rode on alone. She lived in a modern house called Stonecroft on the Waterford road. The remaining seven riders turned right and took the narrow, winding uphill road which led deep into the country. James Morgan was next to go. Calling that he would see them on Wednesday, he turned in at his white gate, beside a huge notice announcing Four Cross Fruit Farm.

The Robertses and the Wheelers jogged on together as the road meandered between fields, ploughed and sown. Smooth green, friendly-looking hills encircled them and far away on the horizon, they could see the blue line of the Downs.

"It's going to be gorgeous having the rallies right on our doorstep," Lizzie told Lynne. "We won't be late any more and Rajah will be much livelier when he hasn't had to hack miles. This morning he was worn out before the schooling started."

"I wonder what David means to do about schools and jumps." Paul sounded worried. "We've got a few poles and drums, but they're not up to much, and James is expecting steeplechase fences."

"He'll have to do something," said Netti. "A rally without jumps would be unbelievably dreary."

"Well, that girl Angela who took the D ride this morning would only let us trot over the poles," said Oliver Wheeler indignantly. "And we spent simply hours touching our toes and going round the world. Not one single race. If this pony club doesn't improve soon I'm going to give up."

"I expect Dad will sort something out," said Lynne comfortably. "He always says he's David's left-hand man and now he's finished with the spring planting and the cattle are out on the hills, the hard work is over until the hay-making starts."

"You'd better tell him that the pony club members will riot," suggested Rupert. "They'll all start chanting and throwing things if they come to a rally and find no jumps. Not that I mind much. Rosie's so completely clueless. I don't think her mother ever told her how to take off."

14

"Do ponies' mothers tell them things?" asked Netti, as the Robertses turned up the Garland Farm lane, leaving the Wheelers to ride on to Kidlake, where they lived in a tumbledown old house that had once been a rectory.

"I suppose you may as well join the pony club if that's what you really want," said Mrs Hutchinson grudgingly as she drove out of Darkwood Lane and took the road to Woodbury. "The subscription's gone up and up since my children were members, and everyone says that the Woodbury Branch is pretty useless. Since Mrs Smythe gave up they haven't done a thing in any of the inter-branch competitions."

"I thought I might make some friends," said Alice Drummond, trying not to be cast down by her Aunt Margaret's perpetual pessimism.

"There aren't many girls of your age round here. The Rookes live on the other side of Woodbury and the Wheelers right out at Kidlake. With petrol so expensive I couldn't possibly keep driving you over there."

"But once we've collected Saffron I won't need driving. I'll be able to ride everywhere," Alice pointed out.

"I can't see the pony tied up outside the dentist's," said Aunt Margaret as the lights changed and they were able to cross the river Vole by the narrow, ancient bridge. "I do hope it's quiet in traffic and easy to catch," she went on, driving past the boat builders and the brewery and the furniture factory, which made up Woodbury's light industries. "Mr Crankshaw has only the one pony and his terms are quite reasonable. I tried Neville Foster at the riding school first, but he charges the earth. And the price of riding lessons nowadays, you wouldn't believe it!"

As they left the town Alice tried to visualise Saffron. A dun Connemara pony, her aunt had told her, fourteen hands one. She had never had a pony of her own. Well, no pets at all. Not a dog or a cat or even a hamster, because her parents had always been on the move. Her father had worked for a multi-national company and they had travel-

15

led the world, never spending more than two or three years in the same place: Washington, Mexico City, Rio de Janerio. She'd ridden a lot at riding schools and then, a year ago, when her parents had sent her back to an English boarding school, she had spent several weekends with pony-owning friends. She had loved catching up the pony and grooming it, having time to talk to it after the ride. It had all been much more fun than an hour's ride at some grand riding school. Now the thought of having a pony for the holidays and looking after it herself seemed the best thing that had happened to her since that cold winter morning when they'd broken the terrible news to her. She remembered the horrified faces and hushed voices of the matron and housemistress as they told her the plane had crashed.

"Ah, this is it, Waterford Farm," said Aunt Margaret, slowing down and turning in at an open gate. As the car sloshed its way up the muddy lane Alice took a look at her aunt's unsmiling face. It always seemed rather grim and aggrieved, pale against the dark red of hennaed hair. She didn't look a bit like Daddy, thought Alice sorrowfully, but then of course she was much older.

While her aunt went to the farmhouse to look for Mr Crankshaw, Alice searched the farm buildings for Saffron. She found him tied in a stall and her first feeling was a shock of disappointment.

She'd been imagining a beautiful pony, with a shining dun coat and a bright eye, but Saffron looked rough and unkempt, his ribs showing through his patchy, half-moulted winter coat, his neck and quarters thin, his eyes wary. Alice gave him a piece of bread and half a carrot as she fought with her disillusionment. Aunt Margaret re-appeared, accompanied by a very tall, thin man. Alice looked up from gumboots, corduroys and macintosh and came to a small face with sticking-out teeth topped by a tweedy cap.

"I'm afraid he's a bit poor," admitted Mr Crankshaw. "He didn't winter too well, but he'll soon pick up now that the grass is coming. I've wormed him and I'll drop in a couple of bags of pony nuts with the hay so that you can feed him up a bit."

Mr Crankshaw looked as though he needed feeding up too, thought Alice, as she patted Saffron and said, "He's lovely."

"I bought him for my younger daughter. She was always moaning that the country was dull and she had nothing to do, but she didn't take to riding. Always hankering after the bright lights, is our Sandra."

"Two of mine were pony-mad for three or four years, then they lost interest," complained Aunt Margaret. "That's what I keep telling Alice. I'm not going to all the expense and bother of buying a pony just to find that she's off on some new craze."

Mr Crankshaw produced a saddle and bridle. "Need a good clean, I'm afraid," he said, looking at them disapprovingly. He handed Alice the snaffle bridle and standing martingale. "He carries his head on the high side so we've always ridden him in a martingale. Do you know how to put it on?"

"Yes, I think so," answered Alice, fumbling nervously. Though she had ridden large horses in covered schools, trekked across plains and climbed rocky hillsides on wiry ponies in foreign lands, she hadn't done much saddling and bridling. Three fingers in the noseband, she reminded herself, and a clenched fist in the throatlash.

"Now, you know the way," said Aunt Margaret, when Alice had mounted. "Out of the yard, through the back gate and follow the track straight down to the river. It's fenced most of the way and you can't miss it because it was once the old road. You cross the river at the ford. I suppose the pony's used to water?" she asked, turning to Mr Crankshaw.

"Oh yes, no problem there. We're up to our knees in it half the winter."

"Then you can see our woods," Aunt Margaret went on. "You follow the track for about three quarters of a mile before you bear left and take a smaller path that'll bring

17

you out in Darkwood Lane. If you don't get lost you'll be home before I am; fighting my way through the town and hanging about at the bridge."

Alice waved goodbye and set off. It was lovely, she thought, as Saffron squelched down the muddy track towards the river, lovely to be riding again, to have a pony as a friend. You didn't miss people so much if you had a pony for company. She patted the thin, dun neck. Saffron seemed very willing. He walked briskly with pricked ears and didn't seem at all worried about setting off into the unknown with a complete stranger. Life on the farm must be very dull, thought Alice. Dull and lonely. Perhaps Saffron was also longing for friends; hoping for some sort of change in the dismalness of his day-to-day life.

The Brunstock Show was turning out to be even more of a misery than Hanif had feared. Jupiter, his handsome liver chestnut pony, was almost delirious with excitement and completely uncontrollable. The riding school's instructions were having no effect. Hot and exhausted, with arms which felt as though they had been pulled out of their shoulder sockets, Hanif longed to give up and go home, but he could here his stepfather's voice calling for him. Tall, fair and very English-looking, Charles Franklin has driven the hordes of gymkhana children away from the practice jump and built it into a solid, three feet six high hog's back.

"Come on, Harry," he called. "Don't mess about, put him straight over."

Hanif abandoned an attempt to circle. He pointed the pony at the fence and, accusing himself of cowardice, took a firm hold of the mane. Jupiter raced for it at terrifying speed and hurled himself over, clearing the top pole by a couple of feet.

"Well done. That's the stuff," shouted Mr Franklin encouragingly. "You'll be all right."

Circling wildly and tugging with all his strength in a hopeless attempt to slow Jupiter down, Hanif knew that his stepfather was being stupidly optimistic.

"Do you know the course? You'd better take another look at the board. You went wrong last Saturday, remember."

"I know the way. The problem is persuading Jupe to take it. I can't stop him except by circling," said Hanif in a despairing voice.

"Oh, for heavens sake! You've got a double bridle and two nosebands. If you can't stop him in that lot you must be as weak as water. Now keep him walking round until they call you. There are two to go, including the girl in the ring."

Hanif sighed with relief as his stepfather strode away to join Mrs Franklin who was watching from the ringside car park. She wasn't like the English mothers, who, with jeans tucked into gumboots, warm in their uniform of head-scarves and green husky coats, sloshed through the mud of the collecting ring, thought Hanif. In her pink and gold Sari and flimsy little shoes she *had* to watch from the car. He was wondering what it would feel like to have an English mother when he heard the collecting steward shouting his number impatiently. "Come on, sixty-three. We're waiting for you and we haven't got all day."

Flustered, apprehensive and with his hands uncomfort-ably full of reins, Hanif trotted into the ring. He didn't see the watching faces of the spectators, only the twelve, huge, brightly-painted fences and the impossible twists and turns he was supposed to make between them. Jupiter's head had disappeared into his chest, but at any minute he would see the jumps and there would be no holding him. Never mind, it'll soon be over, Hanif comforted himself as he turned Jupiter for the brush. With one determined tug the pony snatched control and flung himself at the first jump. Then he raced on, sailing over the gate and parallels with careless contempt. He steadied himself for the combination at the top of the ring, Hanif hauled him round and pointed him diagonally across the wall. They hurtled on, clearing the red wall and rustic gate with ease, but now they had to turn again and they were going far too fast.

"Whoa, boy. Steady," shouted Hanif, tugging on the

19

reins. But there was no response. "Whoa," he called again, pulling on one rein with all his strength and hoping to turn the pony, but they were heading straight for the ring rope at full gallop.

"Look out!" he shouted at the single line of spectators. "Look out, I can't stop!"

For a moment he saw the frightened faces, then Jupiter took off, sailing high into the air. People and ponies scattered, leaving a clear path as they raced on down the showground. It was in the horsebox and trailer park that Hanif finally managed to circle to a halt. He waited for a little to get back his breath and calm his pounding heart. Jupiter, prevented from grazing by his two bits and two nosebands, twirled restlessly.

He'll be furious, Hanif thought despairingly of his stepfather. He won't lose his temper, he won't shout and rage, but he'll be furious inside. He bought Jupe so that I could be a success. He wants to see me beating other fathers' proper English sons, and I'm turning out hopeless. No good at riding or any other sport. It was no good putting things off, he told himself with a sigh, and, turning Jupiter, he rode back slowly.

As he came to the collecting ring he saw a small crowd gathered round an elderly man who was sitting on the ground. Hanif pulled up. "Oh Jupe, *don't* say we hurt someone," he said aloud.

"You didn't kick him or anything, I think he just fell over trying to get out of the way and he's rather ancient," answered a voice, and a thin girl in jeans and a green polo-necked sweater came up and patted Jupiter's neck. "You are an awful pony, jumping out of the ring like that when you were going so well," she told him. "You're a terrific jumper, the way you sailed over those people's heads."

Hanif took a second look at her. She was probably small for her age, he decided. She had a thin, pale face with freckles, faintly red hair that was cut short and curled close to her head, and greenish eyes. She didn't look as though

20

she was despising him for having no control over his pony.

"Is he your own pony?" asked the girl, walking beside him.

"Yes, my stepfather bought him for me at vast expense and now I can't ride him," answered Hanif sadly. "I'm just not up to Jupe's standard. He won a lot with his last owner, so I know it's my fault."

He could see his stepfather's head above the rest of the little group which clustered round the old man.

"Do at least let me drive you home," Charles Franklin was saying.

But the old man was shaking his head. "My daughter and grand-children will look after me," he answered, allowing himself to be helped up.

"Ah, here's the culprit, Harry, come and apologise for yourself," said Mr Franklin, catching sight of his hovering stepson. "You gave poor Mr Orton the fright of his life."

As Hanif said how sorry he was and explained that he couldn't control Jupiter however hard he tried, two of the collecting ring mothers and a very horsey-looking father surrounded Mr Franklin.

"The pony's too big and strong for a boy of his age. You ought to have got him a thirteen-two."

"Or have him taught how to ride the pony before you turn him loose on the unsuspecting public."

"The pony's won a lot in juvenile classes, I bought him with a good reputation," Mr Franklin defended himself. "And my stepson's been having lessons with Mr Foster."

"He's still a public danger. Have you tried the pony club?"

"The Woodbury's not much good. We're lucky, we're all from the Cranford Vale."

"But I've heard that David Lumley, you know, the National Hunt jockey who had a crashing fall at Cheltenham, is taking over the Woodbury, so things may improve."

"And the Secretary's here somewhere, a lady with glasses. She's called Mrs Rooke."

21

"You'd better get off home," Mr Franklin told Hanif, "and for goodness sake keep that pony under control."

Hanif waved goodbye to his mother and set off across the showground. The gymkhana events had started in Ring Two.

"You're going, then?" The small red-headed girl was beside him again.

"Yes, before I do any more damage. Are you riding in the gymkhana?"

"No such luck. I don't have a pony. We couldn't possibly afford one. Besides, we live in a flat. I just biked over with Mr Foster's riding school. I help there sometimes."

"I liked riding at a riding school better. At least I could manage the ponies," said Hanif sadly. "I thought I rode quite well until we moved to Coxwell and I got Jupe."

"Mr Foster's riding school's not much good," said the girl, looking across at the gymkhana ring. "You can see which are *his* pupils. They're all cantering at one mile an hour. They haven't a hope against the people from the Cranford Vale. What's your name?" she asked suddenly.

Hanif thought before he answered. He supposed his stepfather was right, Hanif was too complicated for English people, it was better just to fit in with their ways and call yourself Harry.

"Harry Franklin," he answered. "What's yours?"

"Tina Spencer," answered the red-headed girl, "and I live in Woodbury, in one of those little streets by the river, so, if you *do* join the pony club I may see you around."

CHAPTER TWO

A Disgrace to David

Perhaps the rally will change everything, thought Alice, rubber-curry-combing out huge handfuls of dun winter coat. If only I could make just *one* friend. It's lovely having Saffron but it would be even more fun if I had someone to ride with.

She had tried hard to fit in, but life at Shawbury really was rather dismal. Aunt Margaret was kind in her way, but she was only interested in her dogs. She bred springer spaniels, but they were all kept in kennels with concrete runs and not allowed in the house, so they didn't have much character. And she'd told Alice not to pet them as she might spoil their manners for the show-ring. Uncle Peter was rather fat and dull. He seemed to be interested in stocks and shares and cricket, and never wanted to talk, but hurried home from work and settled down in front of the television. The Hutchinson children, Andrew, Jane, Nick and Clare, were all years older than Alice. Andrew and Jane were working, Nick and Clare still at college. When they came they talked about their jobs and travels and exams. The three older ones couldn't be bothered with Alice, but Clare had been friendly and fun. If only she'd stayed, instead of loading herself with an enormous back-pack and setting out to explore Turkey with a party of friends. Still, Saffron had certainly improved life. Alice had ridden him on every one of the four days for which he had been hers and had spent hours grooming him and cleaning his tack. If only I had had a brother or sister, she thought as she saddled up. It was difficult even to have friends when you moved about the world so much. She had made two at boarding school, but they lived such miles away.

To Hanif, too, it seemed a very important day. If this Mr Lumley can't help, I give up, he thought as he oiled Jupiter's hoofs. Dad will just have to swallow his pride and sell Jupe.

"It's nothing personal," he said, patting the strong, liver chestnut neck. "Just that you're the boss and it ought to be me."

Mrs Franklin, wearing one of her morning saris, came out to the stable as Hanif finished tacking up, and watched as he led Jupiter into the yard and prepared for the usual struggle to mount. She watched helplessly as Jupiter twirled and pranced, and Hanif, one foot in the stirrup, hopped in pursuit. At last he trapped the pony in the corner by the gate and scrambled into the saddle.

"Goodbye, Mum," he shouted, setting off at a hammering trot along the road. "Don't worry, I'll be all right." He knew that such a fast trot was bad for Jupiter's legs, but trying to insist on a slower pace would be hard on his own arms and, anyway, they were late starting. He had never ridden on the far side of Woodbury before and his step-father had said that Hanif would certainly lose himself if he went by the woods and fields and that Jupiter might refuse to ford the river, so there was nothing for it but the long, boring way round by the bridge and the town.

Lesley and Sarah Rooke weren't speaking. Sarah had won a rosette, only a third, in the Twelve and Under Egg and Spoon on Saturday and Mrs Rooke had been bursting with pride ever since.

"The only Woodbury child to come *anywhere*," she told all her friends, "and against the whole of the Cranford Vale Prince Philip B. Team. It was really quite something. I mean, they get to Wembley year after year. But of course Sarah's a natural, good at everything. Poor old Lesley has to learn the hard way. No natural aptitude at all."

It had always been like that, thought Lesley, seething with unspoken resentment as she groomed chestnut Stardust for the rally. Sarah was the pretty one, the clever one,

24

best at everything. Julian was the baby, the boy. He was perfect in Mummy's eyes too. She was the ugly one, no good at anything, the one who didn't count.

She groomed fiercely, too absorbed in her hatred for Sarah to notice Stardust's gentle nuzzling. Only the unsatisfactory things forced themselves upon her attention. Stardust's forelock, which she had cut with scissors, still looked stupidly unnatural and like a fringe, her four white socks were grubby and refused to come clean.

Oh well, what does it matter? she thought angrily. It's only the pony club and no doubt David Lumley will spend his time praising Sarah, telling her what a brilliant little rider she is.

Lesley tacked up, and then finding with pleasure that her sister wasn't ready, started for Garland Farm alone.

Sarah's little piebald, Chess, hated being left behind. He neighed deafeningly, trod on Sarah's toe and refused to keep still while she saddled and bridled him.

Lesley's so jealous. It's mean of her to be so horrible whenever I win anything, thought Sarah, slapping Chess and shouting at him to keep still. It's not my fault if I'm good at things, better than she is. And, anyway, she couldn't win anything when she didn't even enter.

Tina Spencer was bicycling slowly out of Woodbury. It was uphill all the way to Garland Farm, she thought drearily, but still, it didn't matter if she was late, no one noticed the dismounted members. It was her mother who had insisted on her joining the pony club and who had paid her subscription. "Then you'll have something to do in the holidays when I'm working," she had said. And she'd saved the money out of the wages she earned at Fanny's Food and Wine Bar in Cross Street. It hadn't been much fun, standing in cold fields in January and watching other people ride, thought Tina, and she hadn't been able to afford the extra money for the trip to Olympia, but she pretended to her mother that she enjoyed rallies. She didn't want her to know that she had wasted her hard-earned cash. Next year

I'll tell her I'm too old, or something, she decided, as the red town houses ended and the fields began.

Then, hearing frantic neighs, she looked over a hedge and saw Sarah Rooke cantering across the field on an excited and indignant Chess. She leaned her bike against the hedge and opened the gate. "Are you going to the rally?" she asked.

"Yes, and Lesley was in one of her moods and wouldn't wait for me, so now Chess is going mad."

Jennifer Blacker was in a bad mood too. Though she had shouted and sulked and argued for three days she had still not managed to persuade her mother to let her transfer to the Cranford Vale. Mrs Blacker, who was an equally determined character, said that Jennifer needn't go to Woodbury rallies if she didn't enjoy them but that *she* was only prepared to drive her to a show every Saturday, and that was that.

Lesley, seeing Jennifer coming out of the bridle path at Four-cross, slowed up the already dawdling Stardust. She was still seething with anger and she didn't want to ride with anyone. But, as she dawdled along keeping a good distance between herself and Jennifer she heard hoofs and voices coming up from behind and, looking back saw that Sarah and Tina were overtaking her. She kicked Stardust into a trot. But the Rooke ponies were fond of each other, unlike the Rooke sisters. Stardust shuffled slowly, Chess produced his briskest trot and they managed a whinnying reunion as they turned up the Garland Farm Lane.

"Lesley, I forgot to tell you. Mummy says we're to be kind to this new girl, Alice Drummond. Her parents have been killed in an air crash. And there's a new boy too. He's foreign. He's come from Singapore, but he's really a Pakistani." Sarah told her sister.

"*You* can be kind to them," snapped Lesley, her eyes glaring angrily from behind the thick-lensed spectacles. "*You're* the clever one."

Paul was not very happy with the arrangements for the

26

rally. His father had dumped a large number of oil drums, an old pig trough and several worn-out tyres in an untidy heap in Long Meadow. The local builder had delivered six cavaletti and the Forestry Commission twelve immensely heavy fir poles, but there was no course, no steeplechase fences, nothing to impress James. It won't be much fun having a pony club if all the big ones give up coming, he thought despondently as he saddled Banjo.

Lynne was determined that red-roan Berry should be the best-turned-out pony there. She didn't care much about jumping or schooling and the only race she ever won was trotting, but she loved grooming and looking after ponies.

"And for once they're all going to see your oiled hoofs and your freshly water-brushed mane," she told Berry as she polished her with the rubber. "When we had to hack over to Woodbury, Paul said it was all a waste of time, but now it's definitely worth it."

Paul hated grooming, but then they were opposites in most things. He took after Dad and she took after Mum. She looked across at Banjo who was tied to a ring in the cattle-yard wall. His coat was awful. He wasn't losing it properly, and, when he did all the horrible bald patches caused by sweet itch would show up. They'd bought him very cheap because he'd looked so awful, but though they kept him in the yard all through the spring and summer and didn't let him eat a blade of grass, the hair didn't grow again. Luckily Paul didn't seem to mind. Jumping was all he cared about.

Mrs Rooke, the Secretary arrived, bringing Julia Cartwright, one of the junior instructors, who was to take the D ride. Julia was twenty-one, with a plump cheerful face and her brown hair worn in a pony tail. She waited, talking to Lynne and admiring Berry. Mrs Rooke, severely dressed in grey, lay in wait for the members, looking sharply from her watch to her lists and back again.

Suddenly the lane was full of the scrunch of hoofs, and the pony club members came riding past the back of the farmhouse, with its small, square stableyard. Mrs Rooke ticked her list busily, then she found Alice.

"Your badge and fixture card," she said, handing them over. "Now, do be *sure* to put your name down when you are coming to rallies. Is that the pony you've hired for the holidays? He looks a bit poor, you must worm him at once. Now, these are my daughters, Sarah, who's the real rider, and Lesley."

Alice searched her mind desperately for something to say. You didn't make friends by sitting on your pony in stupid silence, but then David Lumley came driving round the corner from his house in a specially adapted Land Rover with a disc announcing 'Disabled Driver' on the rear window. He stopped in the midst of the ponies and people.

Mrs Rooke hurried over. "I'm afraid they're not all here yet," she fussed. "It really is disgraceful."

"Well, let's make a start," said David Lumley. "Can Julia get her ride into the small paddock first?"

He was wearing corduroys, a thick, navy blue polo-necked sweater and a padded waistcoat that was a lighter blue. He sat with the Land Rover door open, but seemed reluctant to get down among the milling crowd of ponies.

"Here come the others," called Lynne, as James, looking unusually hot and flustered, came trotting up the lane, followed by the Wheelers, whose voices, all talking at once, drowned the sound of their ponies' hoofs.

"Late as usual," Lynne taunted them.

"Rupert lost his boots." Lizzie looked round anxiously. "I hope Mr Lumley's not cross."

"I think he is a bit," said Netti, taking a quick glance at the white, unsmiling face. "At least he doesn't look wildly pleased to see us."

"Well, we're not last for once," announced Oliver. "Here's someone arriving at the sideways canter."

"The sideways canter?" Sarah and Lynne hurried to look as a limp, exhausted Hanif and a sweat-lathered Jupiter came clattering into the yard.

"What *have* you been doing to that pony?" demanded Mrs Rooke, eyes glaring behind her glasses. "I've *never*

28

seen anyone arrive at a rally in such a disgraceful condition."

"Sorry," answered Hanif who had no strength left for argument. "He went mad when he saw the other ponies ahead."

Oliver Wheeler, who looked like Rupert, but with a rounder, cheekier face and blue eyes, bright with self-confidence instead of dreamy, began arguing with Mrs Rooke.

"But it's not fair that I should always be in the D ride. I'm only two years younger than Paul and Netti and half the D's are years and years younger than me. Some of them are only six . . ."

"Oh, come on, Ollie," interupted Julia Cartwright. "You know you're my leader and I can't manage without you. And poor David's already got eleven. He can't cope with any more."

Oliver went off to the small paddock, muttering indignantly. David Lumley, trying to escape from an anxious and very talkative mother, shouted to Paul to lead on. Hanif struggled to remount the twirling Jupiter. Alice turned back, grabbed his rein and tried to hold him still.

"Are you new too?" she asked as they rode into their field, which ran, long and narrow, beside the lane and was fenced with thick hedgerows, well studded with trees.

"Yes," agreed Hanif breathlessly, as Jupiter jogged sideways, fighting for his head and, at intervals, pulling his rider half out of the saddle with his violent snatches at the reins. "This is my first rally and I have a feeling it may be my last."

The other riders had been arguing about their positions in the ride, but Hanif and Alice merely joined on at the back. Then, looking across the school at Jennifer on bright bay Sea King followed by James on the stouter, taller, but equally well-turned-out darkbrown Ferdinand, both decided that they were hopelessly outclassed and waited gloomily to be sent to join the D ride.

David Lumley parked the Land Rover in the centre of the school and climbed out slowly.

The pony club members tried to inspect him without staring too obviously as he limped a few steps and then stood, leaning on his shooting stick. He was slim and wiry and about middle height, a good bit taller than some jockeys, thought Alice, who had been to the Jockey Club in Rio de Janerio. His hair was nice, thick, mouse-brown and vaguely curly. His eyes were blue but his face was white and drawn and looked older than the rest of him.

David Lumley looked critically at his pony club members.

The first two looked competent and well-mounted. Behind them came Rupert, gazing into space. His anorak was unzipped, his crash cap on the back of his head and his pony, which was half Exmoor, decided David Lumley, noticing the mealy nose and toad eye, wandered along with its nose poked out. Then there were two girls on chestnuts, one anxiously fiddling with her pony's mouth and looking down, the other dawdling along, sitting in the back of her saddle and not trying at all. A nice-looking little grey led a collection of smaller ponies. Roan Berry, piebald Chess and Black Banjo, all drifted along on each other's tails, while their riders flapped their legs uselessly. At the back came a girl on a stargazing dun, and a liver chestnut, sweating with frustration as he fought his equally unhappy-looking boy rider for his head.

David Lumley sighed. What a collection! he thought. Where *does* one begin?

"Good morning, everyone." He spoke briskly to hide his despondency. I'm David, your new D.C. Now from the front, can you tell me your names. First names will do."

Except for Rupert, who had drifted into a dream and had to be answered for by Lizzie, everyone shouted out his or her name in turn.

"I don't suppose I'll get them all straight off. You'll have to remind me," said David, repeating them. "Now, can we have those two large ponies at the back a bit further forward. Lizzie, would you make a large circle and the rest of you follow her, except for Alice and—was it Harry? Right, you two close up with Rupert. Good. Now prepare to trot on."

They trotted, or at leat the two leaders did. Jupiter, cantering sideways and throwing his head about, was up-setting Rosie and Saffron.

"You'd better keep off my tail. Rosie's not totally reliable, she kicks sometimes," Rupert told Alice, who was trying to sit on the stiff-backed, stargazing Saffron.

"Sorry." She tried to slow the pony up by feeling his mouth, but he simply carried his head higher and higher until his ears were almost in her face. It was a horrible feeling and she seemed powerless; out of control and quite unable to do anything about it.

Suddenly Rosie decided that she had had enough. Taking Rupert by surprise, she opened her mouth wide and charged off down the field in the direction of home. Saffron followed her and Jupiter soon overtook the pair of them and thundered on round the field, ignoring Hanif's tugs and 'whoas'.

Alice stopped first, she managed to circle Saffron and, not being at all fit, he was soon quite pleased to stop cantering round. Red-faced, she hurried back to her place in the ride. Rupert stopped at the far end of the field by riding Rosie into the hedge, and he too slunk back into his place, but everyone was too busy watching Hanif, galloping round the field at full speed and completely out of control, to bother about them.

"Don't worry, just keep him going round until he's tired," shouted David. "Don't bother about stopping, steer."

After four circuits of the field Jupiter showed signs of slowing up. "Keep him going," shouted David. "Go on, round again. You mustn't let him stop the moment he wants to."

He turned to Rupert. "How old is your pony?"

"Six, but she hasn't been schooled."

"I can see that. Are you going to school her?"

"Me?" asked Rupert doubtfully.

"Yes, *you*. Ponies don't school themselves and it's no use hoping for a miracle. If you worked on her for the rest of the summer you might get somewhere."

31

Hanif appeared looking very crestfallen. "Sorry about that," he said to David, "I'm afraid I've no control."

"So I observed. Is your pony stabled?"

"Only at night. He was clipped when we bought him."

"What do you feed him on?"

"Hay, nuts, oats, bran, chaff. The usual things."

"Well, the first thing is to cut out the oats and nuts. Until you've learned to ride him he doesn't get a single oat or nut. Not *one*. O.K.?"

"O.K."

"Right. Number two. Why have you got the wretched animal strapped down like that? Look at you, a double bridle, two nosebands, a curb chain and a running martingale."

"I've never been able to stop him so we've gradually added more and more."

"And you still can't stop him, which proves you're on the wrong track. Let's get some of it off. The dropped noseband and the running martingale to start with, and let the curb chain out a couple of links. "You'll have to do it, I can't. I've got a useless hand."

Hanif dismounted and felt very relieved when Tina appeared to help him.

David had turned his attention to Alice. "How long have you had that pony?" he asked.

"Four days. He's hired for the holidays."

David groaned. "Can you send him back and ask for something rideable?"

"No." Alice shook her head. "I'm afraid not. But he's not as bad as this usually. He's just excited."

"You can cure stargazers, but it takes months rather than weeks," said David with a sigh. "I'm afraid you're in for a rotten holidays."

He turned back to the rest of the ride who were beginning to feel bored and neglected. "Well, now we've got the lunatic ponies under control, let's see what you lot can do. Change the rein, Jennifer. Now I want you to canter on, one at a time, circle at a convenient point and join on at the back of the ride."

Jennifer prodded Sea King into a canter with her heels, circled smoothly and re-joined the ride with a smug expression on her flat, pale face.

David looked at the rest of the ride. "What was wrong with that?" he asked.

"Nothing."

"It was a gorgeously slow canter."

"Perfect," they answered.

"You didn't see anything wrong with the circle?"

"No." They were all shaking their heads.

"Which way should a pony be bent on a circle? Which way should he look?" asked David.

"Inwards," answered Lizzie.

"He should be bent round the rider's inside leg," added Sarah.

"Your turn, James. Now watch carefully this time," David told the members.

"He isn't looking inwards."

"Ferdie's not bent enough."

"Too stiff," they shouted now that they knew what to look for.

Lizzie was next and she had a job to get Rajah cantering. She kicked and whacked energetically and felt quite triumphant when he finally lurched into a canter. "Too fast, he's unbalanced," David was shouting. "Sit up, look up. Take your hands off the withers." Then he waved Lesley on with his good arm. She set off grim-faced and, flapping her legs energetically. She managed to keep Stardust cantering round the school, but the moment she circled the pony fell back into a trot and the rest of the circle was a wild flurry of arms and legs as Lesley tried to get going again.

"No impulsion," shouted David. "It's no use kicking, you've got to sit down and ride. Why's that pony wearing a vulcanite pelham?" he demanded, as Lesley, looking hot and cross, re-joined the ride.

"She always had one she's quite easy to stop in it."

"It's crazy, a pelham on a pony that's behind the bit and

carries its head too low. Don't you understand that with a pelham, whichever rein you use activates the curb chain and therefore has a lowering effect on the pony's head? With a double bridle you have a choice—the bridoon is separate from the curb chain—but your pony needs a snaffle."

"Next," he shouted at Sarah. She was ready and giving Chess a sharp kick broke straight into a canter. She looked down to check that he was on the correct leg, circled neatly and joined the back of the ride.

"Too fast," said David. "Why kick and why look down? We don't want to see your aids. A good rider on a schooled pony gives invisible aids. Only beginners kick."

Netti's little grey Welsh pony, Tristram, had been well-schooled before he belonged to the Wheelers and he went round very neatly, but David said that Netti's circle was more like a banana than a circle and that re-joining the ride was a transition and should be made with elegance. She had stopped with a lurch, using Chess's hindquarters as a buffer.

Lynne made a mess of her turn. Berry trotted faster and further than Rajah, raced round the circle twice and then went half way up the ride before Lynne could stop her.

David sighed. "We know she's been in harness, but you could school her. Hacking may be more fun, but it doesn't improve ponies. You've got to work at it if you want to get anywhere. Go on, Paul."

Paul bustled round on Banjo, who had a very short stride, but was obedient and willing.

"Yes, you do it, but you don't do it well," David told him. "You are all the same," he went on, looking up and down the ride, "You sit on top of your ponies, steering. You kick your heels and you flap your legs and you think you're riding, but you're not. A good rider sits deep, influences the horses hindlegs, gets him moving with impulsion so that he goes on the bit. Some of you are sitting too far forward, some too far back, none of you are sitting deep."

keeping him clam and balanced so that he's in a position to answer them, and then rewarding him when he does so. Your pony knows the signals, he's well-balanced enough to answer, but he isn't calm. All your bits and nosebands have driven him wild with frustration and, because his whole life has become a pulling match, he's never rewarded. He can't change this, ponies don't have the sort of brains that can work out what's gone wrong and what ought to be done about it. That's the rider's job. Now, it takes two to pull and you're *not* going to be one of them. Trot around the school, and if he starts going too fast, circle or change the direction, don't pull."

"A worried looking Hanif was soon circling feverishly as Jupiter, delighted to have his head, tore round and round.

"Do you know how to make a half-halt?" asked David.

"No."

"Can any of you tell him?" asked David, observing the bored faces of the rest of the ride.

"Yes, it's when you nearly halt, but not quite," answered Jennifer.

"That's the idea. By using your legs, back and seat and your hands very lightly, you go through the motions of halting, but the moment the horse obeys you, by putting his hindlegs under him and shortening or collecting, you reward him by giving with the hands. There is no change of pace. With a difficult pony like Harry's you can make a dozen half-halts in one circuit of the school. And, because you are rewarding him each time he obeys he will gradually come to accept your control. Do you understand, Harry? You do *anything* but pull."

"Yes, I'll do my best," answered Hanif in a dispirited voice. This advice didn't seem to be working either, he thought, and the circling was making him giddy.

"Very green ponies like Rupert's, or very stiff ones like Lizzie's, can't half-halt, but the rest of you should use it to get your pony's hindlegs under him and to increase impulsion. Right, form up the ride and let's see if things go better now."

37

The well-behaved ponies cantered and circled in turn while David roared at the riders to 'sit deep'. When Stardust's turn came she was greeted with a shout of triumph. "Look at that pony, she's hardly overbending at all and she's got far more impulsion."

Hanif and Alice, struggling to carry out their instructions, were quite pleased to find themselves ignored as David concentrated on the rest of the ride. He had them all riding a large serpentine, three loops covering the whole school. As they crossed the centre line they were supposed to straighten their ponies and then take up the correct bend for the next loop. Jennifer was roared at for holding her pony out with the outside rein so that he always had a wrong bend. All Lizzie's loops looked like triangles instead of circles and Sarah and Netti were told they were idle, while Paul was sitting crookedly, hanging over one side and trying to force his pony into the correct bend, instead of sitting deep and trying to influence the hindlegs.

Lynne, holding on to the pommel and shrieking that no one could be expected to sit to Berry's trot, simply followed the pony in front, and James, who was also bouncing about and looking hot, was shouted at for always being late in changing his bend and not anticipating.

A general cry of relief went up when at last they were allowed to walk.

"Well, we haven't much time left, and I suppose I'd better see what you're like at jumping," said David. "I'll need some strong characters to haul poles and drums. Could the less strong hold the ponies?"

Except for Jennifer, who immediately offered to hold Ferdinand, everyone wanted to build jumps. Hanif found himself with the Roberts's ponies. Berry took an instant dislike to Jupiter, stamping her fore-foot and squealing if he dared to look at her, and Hanif, being pulled in several directions at once, had to be rescued by Tina.

"She's always awful with strange ponies," shouted Lynne, happily engaged in dragging poles from the Land Rover. "Why don't you ride her round, Tina?"

A delighted Tina rushed round trying to find a crash cap to fit her. Sarah's was almost the right size and she mounted and rode proudly away round the field.

Hanif watched dismally as the course emerged. The jumps were nothing like the size he was expected to jump at home, they were only about two-feet-nine in height, but there were all the usual fatal twists and turns. But, when the course was ready and everyone was mounting, David drove over in the Land Rover and said, "We've put three cavaletti in the centre of the school for the lunatic ponies. I don't think it's any use trying to jump them at the moment. You're just going to undo any improvement you've made this morning."

The other riders, excitedly shortening their stirrups, looked at the banned three with shocked pity. But Hannif was ashamed at his feeling of relief and Alice announced firmly that jumping inside out would be no fun at all and she liked cavaletti work.

They trotted round and round, changing the rein at intervals. At first the ponies were excited. Saffron stargazed, Jupiter tried to rush at the poles and fling himself over, Rosie tried to avoid the whole business by charging past them, but gradually the steady trotting round and round calmed them, they began to lower their heads, round their backs and even Rosie, to Rupert's delight, produced a slow cadenced trot.

When they felt the ponies had done enough they stopped and watched the jumping. It was a good course, very solid-looking, with the pig trough, tyres, straw bales and a log making the various arrangements of poles and drums more interesting. But David didn't sound very satisfied with the standard of riding.

"You're all far too busy," he was shouting. "*You* don't have to get the pony over. Your job is to get him going in a balanced manner and with plenty of impulsion. Let *him* do the jumping. Sit *still*. How can a pony concentrate on jumping if you're kicking and steering right up to the fence? Get him going properly before you put him at it. You all ride like beginners. I don't want to see your aids. Use your legs *quietly*, in time with his stride."

Finally he sent them round the course one behind the other, with instructions to keep going and jump every fence three times.

"They do look a bit wild," observed Hanif, watching them critically. Alice felt a huge pang of envy. She did long to be flying round there too.

As David dismissed the ride and then limped to the Land Rover, Mrs Rooke came hurrying down the field.

"I've an announcement to make, David," she called. "Quite an important one."

"You carry on," answered David, going through the awkward, twisting motions that would get him into the driver's seat.

"Listen, everybody," Mrs Rooke commanded the members. "As you know, the pony club is divided into Regions, Areas and Branches and I've just received a letter from our Area Representative telling me about a new competition which is to take place these holidays. It's intended for younger members and those who don't have good enough ponies for the main inter-branch events; in fact, anyone representing their branch in the horse trials or Prince Philip is ineligible. It's to be called the Area Cup, and each team competes in all the phases: dressage, cross-country, turnout and quiz, but there are five members in each team and only four perform in each phase. I thought it sounded just the thing for us."

"*These* holidays?" asked David from the Land Rover.

"That's right."

"Not a chance. None of them can ride a circle yet, much less a dressage test, and their jumping's abysmal. We don't want to disgrace the Woodbury the moment we take over. Give me a year and I'll produce a reasonable team." He started the engine. "Goodbye everyone. See you next week. And *please* school those ponies."

He drove away up the field, leaving them all too surprised to shout their thank yous for the rally.

40

"Well, he won't see *me* next week," said Jennifer indignantly.

"Oh dear, he was rather brusque. I do hope he hasn't overdone things. He did look rather grey," worried Mrs Rooke, starting after the departing Land Rover. "I hope he's well enough to take on the job of D.C."

"Yes, and some of us could perfectly well go in for this cup," Jennifer went on, her indignation rising. "I know half the ride was completely useless. There ought to have been another instructor to stop them holding things up and spoiling it for the rest of us, but we could make up a team of five, Mrs Rooke."

"You, James, Sarah," agreed Mrs Rooke, "and then I suppose Netti and perhaps a Roberts. Yes, I'll talk it over with David again when he's less tired."

The other members were looking at each other despondently.

"He doesn't think much of us," said Lizzie sadly.

"He thinks we're dim."

"Dim and wet."

"Well, I'm afraid we didn't put on a very good show," James admitted solemnly.

The D Ride had finished earlier and only Oliver Wheeler waited in the yard. Everyone else had gone home.

"We had a great time," he announced. "Hobbit won the Handy Pony and Musical Sacks and my lot won the Relay. How did you get on?"

"Ghastly," answered Rupert sliding off Rosie. "My legs are in a state of collapse from overwork and I don't think this silly pony's improved at all."

"It takes time," Lizzie told him. "And the noseband did help a bit."

Hanif dismounted. "Would it be all right to eat lunch here, before starting home?" he asked Lynne.

"Yes, of course. Would you like to water your pony at the trough? It's over there. And, if you haven't got a headcollar I'll lend you Berry's and you can tie him up while you eat."

41

"Thanks." Hanif took off his crash cap and rumpled his thick, blue-black hair. "What about the noseband, Rupert? Would you like to keep it for a bit?" he asked.

"Well, yes, if you don't need it. Can I borrow it until next Wednesday? If it really works I may be able to persuade my parents to buy me one, but it won't be easy. They're a bit broke at the moment."

"What about your pelham?" Alice asked Lesley.

"I don't care one way or the other. I can't see that it's made much difference to Stardust."

"Well, if you really don't mind, can I keep it?" asked Alice. "I think it really does make quite a big difference to Saffron."

Only Hanif and Alice stayed to eat their lunches. Tina wished she had thought of bringing hers. I will next week, she decided, as she bicycled down the lane behind the Wheelers. Everyone was much friendlier this time and Lynne let me ride Berry.

"Do you live a long way away too?" asked Hanif, as, with the ponies tied up and munching the wisps of hay scattered over the barn floor, he and Alice collapsed on straw bales and unpacked their food.

"Yes, Darkwood Lane. It's on the other side of Woodbury, but my aunt's taught me all the short cuts so it's a lovely ride. All woods and fields until you get to Four Cross."

Hanif, looking at Alice's face, decided that he liked her. She wasn't a pink and white English blonde like the Wheelers. Her hair was dark gold, her skin brownish, her eyes dark blue. She had a big mouth, a straight nose and a decided expression. She looks Swedish, he thought.

"I live at Coxwell," he told her. "It's not far from you, so perhaps you'll show me the good way home. I wasn't sure that I'd ever get Jupe to ford the river so I came all the way by road."

CHAPTER THREE

We Need Advice

After the rally, Mrs Rooke was very anxious that Sarah should school.

"David did ask that you should all train your ponies, and we do want you in top form," she said. "I know there isn't much time, but supposing I did persuade him to relent and at least *consider* entering for the Area Cup, you must have Chess going well. Perhaps you should go round to Mr Foster's. I know the instruction's not up to much, but you have the use of the jumps and the dressage arena, and if you have your own pony they only charge a third of the cost of a proper lesson."

So, next morning, Sarah went off to the riding school, and Lesley, who had paid more attention to David's advice than she had admitted, doubled the oats and nuts in Stardust's feed and made two jumps out of straw bales and a old door. Later on, when Stardust had digested, she had pulled up her stirrups and tried going round the field at the gallop.

"Inspire that pony," David had said. "Don't kick her, get her going with impulsion. She's a nice-looking pony. She shouldn't be dawdling along behind the bit. Go on, wake her up. Make something of her."

Well, at least he hadn't told Sarah that she was a brilliant little rider. He had swept aside Mummy's suggestion that Jennifer, James and Sarah were better than the rest. That had kindled a faint spark of hope in her. I'll try for a week, she decided, and then, if he doesn't notice, I'll go back to hacking.

Alice had shown Hanif the way home by the Four Cross bridle path, Waterford Farm and the woods. They hadn't talked much because they had both been worn out by the rally, and she was very surprised when Hanif telephoned next morning at breakfast-time.

"Are you going to school today?" he asked, "because if you are, why not come over and ride in our field? I've got some jumps and a school marked out. Jupiter keeps neighing. I think he's missing his pony club friends."

"Oh, terrific," said Alice, who knew that Aunt Margaret was sighing over the muddy track she was making in the paddock. "Shall I come as soon as I've groomed?"

"Yes, that'll be great," Hanif sounded pleased. "See you."

When Alice arrived, Hanif was attempting to mount a spinning Jupiter. Saffron, excited by his lively companion, followed them out to the field stargazing horribly.

"Oh, what lovely jumps," Alice exclaimed, amazed at the sight of six professional-looking show jumps arranged in the centre of the field. "You are *lucky*."

"Am I?" asked Hanif, already hot and harrassed by Jupiter's behaviour. My stepfather's bought me a brilliant pony which I can't ride and made me perfect show jumps which I can't jump. Well, not properly. I crash over out of control." He sounded very bitter and despairing.

"Does he know anything about riding?" asked Alice, walking round the school and admiring the letters which marked it, neatly painted on white plastic buckets.

"A bit. He belonged to the pony club when he was a boy. He was in the tetrathlon team. I think he was better at running and shooting and swimming than at riding, but he's good at all sports."

"Tough," said Alice. "On you, I mean. Still, he seems very generous."

"Yes, but then I feel I'm letting him down," explained Hanif. "If he gave me less I might not feel such a failure."

"Well, I'm afraid I'm a great trial to my relations too," said Alice, glad to tell someone. "You see my aunt and uncle thought they had finished with children. Theirs are all grown-up, the youngest is twenty, and now they've had to give me a home. My mother was an only child and my

44

father had this one, much older sister, so she feels she has to take me in. Things are a bit better now I've got Saffy. At least I can go for long rides. I'm not under my aunt's feet *all* day."

"Our lives are full of problems," said Hanif, "and you ponies should help us, not add to them. Do you hear, Jupiter? Now do stop messing about and walk on a loose rein."

They schooled at the walk. Alice was pleased with Saffron. The pelham was being a great help and she could almost always keep his neck the right way round walking and halting. Jupiter was still jogging and looking round for excitement. He still seemed over-fresh, but gradually he calmed down and began to walk on a long rein.

When they were tired of walking they agreed to try a trot. Jupiter set off immediately at a sideways canter and Saffron, catching his sense of excitement, began to star-gaze. Alice walked, halted and started again, this time smoothly and on a circle. She practised circles on both reins and then, becoming bolder, attempted a serpentine.

Hanif, tired of battling with his snatching, bouncing pony, stopped for a rest and stood in the centre, watching her.

"You're doing quite well," he said. That's a big improvement. When Saffy's going properly he looks quite a superior sort of pony."

"It's partly the bit. He's not afraid of it in the same way that he was of the snaffle. I suppose being large and round and not having a joint it feels quite different."

"When you're worn out, will you stop and watch me?" Hanif said. "I'm not getting anywhere and you may be able to see what I'm doing wrong."

Alice's legs were already aching. She had to squeeze so hard to keep Saffron on the bit, and glad of an excuse for a rest, she halted carefully, beside Hanif.

"He's not bad at the walk. Look." Hanif set off round the school on a long rein.

"You see, I'm giving him his head at the walk, no problems, but when we try trotting . . ." He picked up the reins and a pulling match began. Soon Jupiter was cantering sideways and flinging his head about.

"Try circling," said Alice. But Jupiter merely proved that it was possible to circle at a sideways canter. Swinging his quarters he bounced round and round until Hanif began to wrench at the reins angrily.

"Walk," said Alice. "Try and get him to relax again."

"It's no use," Hanif sounded despondent. "The same thing happens every time."

"But supposing you start off with a completely loose rein, exactly as though you were walking. Don't shorten them this time. Leave them lying on his neck and start off very gently."

"I'll probably gallop twice round the field," said Hanif gloomily. "Trot on, Jupe."

Jupiter started fast, but then he seemed confused to find he had nothing to pull against. He gradually settled to a shambling trot with his head low.

"It feels very peculiar, unbalanced," said Hanif, "but it's restful for the arms. Though how I'm supposed to circle or jump like this is beyond me."

"It's beyond me too," agreed Alice. "But I should go on riding like that. At least he's stopped being a fiery charger."

They schooled on. Experimenting, Hanif found that he could persuade Jupiter to walk or halt by word of mouth and taking his weight back and he could make vague circles with a slight feel on the inside rein.

"I don't see what the next stage is," he said when they both stopped for a rest. "I suppose I can go on trotting round like this until next Wednesday."

"We need more advice. We're doing what David told us and it's working, but we need to be told what to do next. Do you think he'd take another look at us?"

"Before Wednesday?"

"Yes."

"It's asking a lot. I don't think he enjoyed teaching us, we were too awful. I think he'll just say no."

That wouldn't kill us," said Alice. "Do you think if he knew we were really *serious* about schooling he might agree to help us?"

"I don't know," answered Hanif. "We've only met him once and we didn't really get to know him."

"The Robertses know him best. We might ask them what they think," suggested Alice. "And if Rupert and Lizzie are trying to school they may be desperate for advice too. I'd telephone them all, only Aunt Margaret's in a great fuss about her bill. Why don't we ride over? Are you doing anything tomorrow?"

"No, just trying to tame Jupe."

"Will you come then? We could take our lunches. Let's visit Lizzie and Rupert first, and if they agree we'll ask the Robertses whether we dare ask David. We don't want to put him off the pony club altogether."

It was a sunny April morning with a pale blue sky and small scudding clouds. A good omen, thought Alice, looking up through the still bare branches of the beech trees as she waited in the lane for Hanif. Aunt Margaret was training one of her dogs, walking it up and down the paddock and making it stand at attention in front of imaginary judges. They both looked rather bored.

Hanif came down the lane, walking on a loose rein. "Sorry I'm late," he said. "I didn't dare try trotting."

Along the narrow path through the wood both ponies wanted to lead, and whichever was behind jogged and pulled or jogged and stargazed, but once they had crossed the river and could walk side by side up Mr Crankshaw's muddy track, they settled down.

The Wheelers' house was old, and it peered out from beneath a mass of ivy. Half-attached trellises dangled from its walls, unsupported creepers and climbing roses grew downwards instead of up. They rode into the cobbled yard at the side of the house. The stable doors sagged on their hinges and needed painting. Headcollars, buckets and grooming tools lay scattered everywhere.

It was very different from Harry's weedless gravel, clipped hedges and perfect loosebox, thought Alice. Very different from Shawbury with its gloomy, dripping trees and the smell of dogs' meat cooking. She liked it better.

"I can hear their voices," said Hanif. "Do you think we should look for them down there?"

They took a path through the overgrown laurels and came to a field. It was a very bald field. The grass was eaten right down to the earth, and it was scattered with bits of jumps and battered oil drums. Rupert was riding Rajah and Lizzie Rosie. They seemed to be schooling earnestly.

"You're right, he is like a board," shouted Rupert. "In some ways he's worse than Rosie."

"She's so *long*, she seems to go on for ever," Lizzie shouted back. "I've tried everything, but I can't seem to push her together!"

Lizzie was looking down with a worried expression, completely absorbed by her schooling. It was Rupert who saw Alice and Hanif at the gate.

"Visitors," he shouted, obviously welcoming any interruption. Kicking Rajah into a canter, he came thundering over. "As you can see we're obediently schooling. But, as you may also have noticed, we are not making much impression."

"We've improved a bit," Alice told him. "We can both walk, but we need more advice. We can't wait until Wednesday."

"It's no use coming here for advice," said Lizzie, arriving at a fast, unbalanced trot. "We need it more than anyone else."

"We hoped you might be feeling desperate too." Alice looked at Hanif.

"What Alice means is, do we have the courage to ask David for another schooling session for the lunatic ponies before next Wednesday," said Hanif quickly.

"Oh, we *can't*." Lizzie sounded horrified at the idea. "He was quite worn out by the last one. And we were all so dreadfully bad. I don't think he liked teaching us one bit."

48

"I was afraid you would say that," admitted Alice sadly.

"Of course, you could make out a case that it's in his own interest," said Rupert. "I mean, if we improve we won't be so ghastly to teach and we won't drive him potty. Once we're all riding well on our beautifully schooled ponies, he'll be able to hold up his head among the other D.C.s."

"But you can't possibly ask for an extra rally," objected Lizzie.

"No, not a rally, just advice. I can walk and trot on a loose rein. What do I do next?"

"My question's about the canter, I can keep Saffy on the bit at walk and trot, but he turns inside out the moment we canter," added Alice.

"I still don't understand what to do about Rosie's nose. I've schooled her all morning and if anything its worse, so I could certainly do with advice if there's any going," said Rupert.

"We could consult Lynne and Paul," suggested Alice. "They know David best."

"Yes, let's do that," agreed Rupert. "Anything to stop schooling. Here, take your ramrod Ra, Lizzie. I think he's un-bendable and you've got to accept a lifetime of square circles."

"No, I won't give up," Lizzie answered firmly. "I'm sure Ra is really as good as all the other ponies. It's probably just me."

They rode back down the winding road towards Garland Farm.

"It's lovely here," said Alice looking at the primroses on the banks and the circle of smooth green hills.

"It's a great place for riding. Netti and Ollie have gone for a gallop up Beacon Hill." Lizzie pointed. "The tall one, over there. But of course the beech woods are best in the summer; cool and shady and the ground doesn't get so hard."

As they drew nearer to the farm they all became silent, for the favour they were about to ask seemed to be growing larger, while the importance of their reasons for asking it

49

was shrinking to nothing. They found Lynne and Paul painting their jumps. They had the poles propped along the fence and Lynne was painting sections in white, Paul in red, both leaving spaces for the other colour to go on later. They seemed very pleased to see the pony club members.

"We thought we'd smarten things up a bit for Wednesday," Paul explained, "and since David bought rustic poles, we thought we'd have ours coloured."

"Has he recovered from the rally?" asked Alice.

"Looks like it. He's been round the farm in the Land Rover this morning," Paul answered.

"He told Mum he was absolutely whacked after coping with us lot, but I think he's over it now," added Lynne.

"Where is he?" asked Rupert, looking round the farm buildings.

"Gone for his lunch, I should think. It's half-past-twelve."

"We can't disturb him at lunchtime," said Lizzie, glad to grab at any obstacle.

"We've come to ask him for some more advice," Alice explained. "We've all been doing the things he told us and we've improved a bit, but now we've all run into new problems and we've got questions to ask. It'll be a terrible waste of time to wait until next Wednesday."

"And when he's got a whole ride he can't spend much time on us, it holds everything up," added Hanif.

The Robertses looked at each other. "Mum's always telling us we mustn't bother him," said Lynne, but you're the pony club and that's different. If you like I'll pop round and tell him you're here."

"Yes, and you might explain that we've come for advice," Rupert told her.

"And that we've brought our lunches so we don't mind waiting until it's convenient," added Hanif.

Lynne ran round the corner of the dutch barn and vanished.

"It looks a nice house, old," said Hanif, studying the back, for it had been built to face south and the Downs.

"Yes, it's very old," Paul sounded quite proud. "And David's made it very posh inside. He was going to get married, you see. Everything was settled and then he had the accident. His girlfriend chucked him when he was in hospital. It was when they thought he would never be able to walk again."

"What a horrible girlfriend," said Lizzie indignantly.

"Dad always thought she was a good-looker, but Lynne and I didn't like her much. Mum says David's well out of it," added Paul.

"Poor David, he must have been miserable. That on top of everything else," said Alice, "though I suppose you've got to look at it from her side too."

"Well, at the time he was fighting to get better. He was determined to get out of his wheelchair. Dad used to go and see him in hospital. He said he was really brave. Then, when he got home it all seemed to hit him, and he got really depressed."

"It was a good thing he'd bought the farm and lucky he'd got all of you," said Alice.

"Well, jockeys don't go on for ever, so, if they've any sense they save when they're doing well and buy a place where they train a few horses later, when they retire. David's got a row of boxes by the house. But now no one knows whether he'll be capable of training. The kick he got on the head is the worst of it. His brain was damaged and that's why his left arm doesn't work and he still gets headaches."

"He's welcome to use us as guinea-pigs," said Hanif.

"It's quite different training racehorses to teaching the pony club," Paul began, but Alice interrupted him.

"Here's Lynne coming back."

"He says he'll come and see you in about twenty minutes to half an hour when he's had lunch," Lynne told them.

"How did he take it?"

"Did you tell him we wanted advice?"

"Did he seem cross?" they asked, crowding round her.

"I don't know really. He seemed a bit put out to start

51

with, but then he said O.K. and went on cooking his chops. Everything takes him such a long time with only one hand that works, but he doesn't like it if you keep offering to help."

The pony club members looked at each other doubtfully. It didn't seem very hopeful.

"Oh well, we'd better eat our lunches," said Hanif despondently. "Can we tie the ponies to the barn, Lynne?"

Hanif was packing his picnic box away in his rucksack when David appeared round the corner of the barn. His limp looked even worse than on Wednesday, thought Alice, trying not to stare. His walk was a sort of crabwise movement. Perhaps they really ought not to bother him.

"You wanted to see me?" asked David, sitting down on the nearest hay bale.

"Yes," they all answered at once, and then they stood round speechless, each hoping that someone else would begin.

Alice took the plunge. "We've been schooling, doing all the things you told us, and the ponies have improved a bit, but now we need more advice and next Wednesday's such a long way off. We wondered, well, if you could take another look at us and our ponies."

"Just to see if we're on the right track," Hanif added hastily, "and where we go next. I've got Jupiter to walk and trot on a loose rein, but I've no control and I don't see how it works show-jumping."

"And I've cornered and circled Rajah for hours, but it doesn't seem to be doing much good so I can't be doing it properly," wailed Lizzie.

"And I can go round and round the school now. We don't charge off at all, but Rosie doesn't show the smallest sign of going on the bit," complained Rupert.

"Three of you were the lunatic fringe, weren't you?" asked David. "I seem to recognise the worst behaved of the ponies."

"Yes, I'm afraid so," agreed Alice sadly. "But we are determined to improve. We've all been schooling very seriously."

David looked round at their doleful faces and suddenly smiled. "All right, you've convinced me. I didn't expect to see any of you again after the rough time I gave you on Wednesday, but if you're that keen I'd better try to help. We'll go in the small paddock and take a look at all these problems."

"Oh thanks."

"Great," they said, rushing to buckle nosebands and tighten girths.

"Could someone fetch my shooting stick from the Land Rover?" asked David as they mounted.

"I will." Lizzie trotted off towards the house and returned in a few moments, bearing the stick proudly. "You go on and start walking round," said David, getting to his feet painfully.

The riders were all grimly intent on showing improvement, but the ponies were excited and uncooperative. Saffron was jogging and stragazing, Jupiter fighting for his head. Alice turned away from the others and circled, Hanif rode round in the opposite direction from the Wheelers and dropped his reins. David reached the centre of the paddock and sat watching them.

Then he said, "Look, they're all so completely different I think I'd better see you one at a time. Alice first. The rest of you come into the centre and watch."

Alice circled, using her legs desperately, determined to prove that she could keep Saffron's head down at the walk, whatever happened at the trot.

"You've got the idea," David called to her. "He's happier in that bit and you've persuaded him to accept your contact with his mouth. But you must remember that it's difficult for him to carry his head the correct way, you've got to allow time for the muscles to develop. When they do, everything will become easy for him, but until then you must give him frequent rests. After every spell of going on the bit, give him a spell of walking on a long rein, let him stretch his neck right out."

"Supposing he puts it up?" asked Alice.

"If he's calm he won't. But go on, give him a long rein now. Good. This applies to all of you." David turned to the stationary riders. "When you've schooled for, say, ten minutes, give your pony a long rein and if he walks round stretching out his neck as Saffron is, that shows your schooling has been on the right lines."

He gestured towards Alice. "Keep him going. It's his neck muscles we're resting, not your legs. Remember that on a lively pony you must use your legs very quietly every stride. Now, pick up your reins, very gently, put him back on the bit and, when you're ready, try a trot."

Saffron threw up his head and set off at his jerky stiff-backed trot.

"Keep rising," shouted David. "It's no use trying to sit on a stiff-backed pony, you only make him worse. Use your legs together as you touch the saddle. No, it's no use. You've lost him. Come back to a walk and try again. Now this time I want you to squeeze your inside rein in time with your legs. Give a squeeze at the same moment as you ask him to trot. The idea is to keep his jaw soft and flexed, to persuade him not to stiffen or resist as he changes pace. The trouble about horses is that their jaws, necks, backs and hindlegs are all attached and if anyone of them is stiff the whole lot are affected. Off you go, Alice, and keep squeezing." He let her trot around several times.

"Well done, now see if you can change the rein through the circle and go round the other way. Good, you've got the idea. And I'm afraid that you've simply got to go on and on like that until he developes the right muscles. It's a long and boring business."

"I don't mind said Alice, patting the dun neck. "I've got nothing else to do these holidays so I may as well try to re-school him even though he's not mine."

"Right, well we'll have Rupert next. Bring that pony over here, I want to have a look at the noseband. Good grief!" he went on indignantly. "You've pulled it up so tight she *can't* flex her jaw. Of course she's not going on the bit, you've made it impossible."

"I thought they weren't supposed to open their mouths," said Rupert, his pink and white face flushing scarlet. "I thought that was the whole point of a dropped noseband."

"No, it's to stop them opening their mouths *wide* and evading the bit. To have a soft mouth and a supple spine a pony must flex or relax his jaw and gently chew his bit. Jump off and let it out. You must leave room for three fingers."

"You all seem to have the idea that if a little of something is good, more of it must be better," he complained, as Rupert re-mounted and began to walk round. "It's not true. We want as few gadgets and bits as possible. We want to use the lightest possible aids. We want to make everything look easy and simple. That's the sign of a good rider."

"But lots of leg," suggested Alice.

"No, not more than is necessary. None of you have learned to use your legs and seats properly yet. You're not 'active' riders. Everyone is a beginner for at least two years and then, as you become more experienced, you have to change into an active rider, who influences his horse, instead of just sitting on him. Once we've got you all riding forward, using your legs and seats automatically, and you've developed the right muscles, it won't be such an effort."

He turned to Rupert. "Leave her nose alone. Stop thinking you can *pull* it in. Ride her forward, think about her hindlegs. If you get them working she'll start to improve. Your hands *feel* her mouth, but they follow it. There musn't be any backward pull. You wouldn't ride a bicycle pedalling like hell with the brakes on, would you?"

When Rupert began to look exhausted he was called in and Lizzie took his place. They could all see how stiff Rajah was on the circle, and Lizzie, looking down, seemed to have become equally tense and rigid.

"Relax," David shouted at her. "Loosen your elbow joints, stop fixing your hands on his neck. You won't get anywhere if you try to *force* him into the correct position, in fact you'll make it more difficult. Relax, put your reins in one hand, look at the scenery." When he had Lizzie and Rajah both looking less tense, David called them in.

"Your pony has been spoiled," he said. He's not like your brother's youngster, who's just green and unschooled. He's acquired bad habits and being middle-aged he's set in his ways. You can't *force* him into another shape, force him to bend his ribs, but with suppling exercises we can certainly improve him. Have you heard of shoulder-in?"

Lizzie nodded.

"Well I think he'd find that too difficult at the moment, so I'd like to start with something called leg-yielding. It's quite simple," he added as Lizzie's expression became anxious. "Just walk round on the circle, now turn his head in a little more with your inside rein and at the same time push his quarters out with your inside leg. No, no, no. Sit up, look up, relax your elbows. If you stiffen up and sit badly you make it harder for him. All right, ride on, and when you've come round the circle, try again.

Lizzie had to struggle so hard against her own habits of looking down, leaning over and stiffening her elbows, that she couldn't do much about Rajah, and the more David looked at her the stiffer and more self-conscious she became. He turned back to the others.

"Rosie's not ready for this yet, but let's try the dun. Walk him round on the same circle as Lizzie and when you've got him going nicely, increase the feel on the inside rein and push his quarters out, just for a couple of steps."

Saffron was good at it and Lizzie, seeing that it could be done, stopped worrying and suddenly Rajah got the idea.

"Well *done*," shouted David in tones of triumph. "Did you feel that? He took and extra large step with his hindleg and at the same moment flexed his jaw. That's what we want. Give him a pat and then try again. You see it's the inside hindleg coming under the body and taking the weight that *enables* them to bend."

He told the two girls to practise on the other rein while he looked at Jupiter, and Hanif set off, holding his reins at the buckle and pleading with Jupiter to behave.

"Well, that's certainly an improvement," announced David. "What about the trot?"

"We sort of lumber round," answered Hanif, gingerly urging Jupiter into a gentle jog.

"Good, you've taught yourself not to pull at him. Now you've got to acquire control by using the legs."

"Legs?" repeated Hanif. "We'll be off down the field if I do."

"That's another bad habit then," said David. "You can't let your pony think that legs only mean 'go faster'. They don't, they also mean 'put your hindlegs further under you', 'go slower, but more collectedly', and, as we tried to teach him the other day, 'half-halt'. You can't do anything with a pony that runs away from the leg. We have to teach him to accept it, just as we have to teach him to accept the bit. Now start using each leg in turn at the walk, slowly in time with his stride. Never mind if he jogs, tell him to walk. Relax, give him a pat, go on using your legs. Now pick up your reins, very quietly, go on using your legs. You've got to ride him forward. Forward, on to the bit. Try a halt, and again remember to ride him *forward* into the halt. Your hands and your weight give him the signal, but there's no pulling. You go on riding him forward and finally he stops. Do you begin to understand?"

"Yes, I think so," said Hanif doubtfully.

"Well, you carry on schooling, I'll just watch. Use your legs one at a time when walking, both together at the trot, and don't attempt cantering for the moment. The trot is much the best pace at which to school."

Presently he called them all over. "Well, that's enough for to-day. I'm sure they've all got aching muscles and I hope you have. Are you pleased with them?"

"Yes." Alice spoke first. "He's going far better at the trot and he loves leg-yielding."

"I *think* I'm beginning to see a faint glimmer of light at the far end of the tunnel." Hanif didn't seem very certain. "But I still can't quite see myself jumping round a ring under control."

"Nor can I," agreed David. "The answer is don't attempt to jump until you can ride him on the flat."

"Is it all right if I tell my stepfather that you say I'm definitely not to enter any more shows for the moment? You see, he thinks I'm being wet, but he regards you as an expert. He'd take it from you."

"That's big of him," said David. "Well, tell him that I'd rather you didn't show-jump until I've sorted the pair of you out, and that to do so will only delay the sorting-out process."

He turned to the Wheelers "Lizzie did you get anywhere?"

"Yes. Ra's bending a tiny bit and he's chewed his bit several times and he's got the idea of leg-yielding."

"Rosie's still pretty ghastly," complained Rupert.

"She's young. You can produce quicker results with a spoiled horse; a young one always needs plenty of time. The trouble with you is that you go round and round in a dream, boring the pants off your pony. Do try and think what you're aiming for and practise energetically for short spells. Think of yourselves as teachers and then see how you rate. I see Alice as a bit too demanding, Rupert as droning on and on, putting everyone to sleep, and Lizzie so uptight about it all she makes her pupils feel that they'll never make it."

"What about Harry?" asked Rupert.

"I haven't decided about him yet."

"David." Paul, who had been waiting for his chance, braced himself to speak. "I suppose you couldn't give us *all* some extra lessons, could you? I know our ponies aren't really difficult, but we would like to improve."

"Yes, so would Netti." Lizzie spoke up for her sister. "And I'm sure the Rookes would love to have some lessons too."

"What about training us for this new cup?

I don't mean that we should *enter*, I know we're not good enough for this year, but it would give us something to *work for*," said Lynne in very diplomatic tones. She'd discussed the whole matter with her mother.

58

David looked around at their serious faces. "You mean that you're not content with a rally once a week?" he asked.

"No. Four rallies in the Easter holidays don't get you anywhere," complained Rupert.

"The Cranford Vale have a week's camp in the summer and three-day courses as well as the ordinary rallies," added Lizzie, who'd seen Jennifer Blacker's fixture card.

"We'll never be as good as them, but I'm sure we'd improve with training," observed Lynne.

"If we're going to train for this cup we'd need a cross-country course and a dressage arena," David pointed out. "Who's going to do all the work?"

"We would," answered Paul in a determined voice. "You and Dad could tell us what to do and I know James would help if it was cross-country, and he's very strong."

"Yes, we'd all help," agreed Lizzie, and Hanif and Alice made assenting noises.

"We might do something on Coppice Hill, I suppose," said David thoughtfully.

"It's a bit rough and steep up there, isn't it?" Paul sounded dubious.

"That's the whole point. You can't do cross-country on the flat. Look, leave it with me. I'll talk it over with Mrs Rooke and if we decide to go ahead she'll telephone you all. O.K.?"

"Yes," Paul nodded, trying to hide his disappointment. He couldn't see Mrs Rooke agreeing.

"And thank you very much for today," said Lizzie.

"Yes, it's been a great help."

"Thanks a lot."

"Pleasure," said David. "You go on, I'll follow slowly."

Hanif collected his rucksack. The Wheelers and Alice said goodbye to Paul and Lynne and then the four of them clattered away down the lane.

"I wish Paul and Lynne hadn't brought up this cup business again," said Hanif. "I was going to ask if we could come again for another lesson, but now I'm sure he'll be put off by the thought of dressage arenas and cross-country jumps."

"I thought he rather liked the idea of cross-country. His face brightened at the thought of Coppice Hill, wherever that may be," said Alice.

Rupert stood in his stirrups and pointed over the hedge with his whip. "It's that hill, over there, with the round wood on the top. It's never ploughed. Too rough or too steep, I suppose."

Hanif looked across the flat, orderly fields, shaded in different greens by their various crops, to the rising hills. "That one?" he asked, pointing in horror. "You'll never see me or Jupe again if we have to go up there."

CHAPTER FOUR

Coppice Hill

It was Sarah Rooke who telephoned the pony club members.

"Message from David," she told them. "He's willing to start training for next year's Area Cup and there will be cross-country sessions at Garland Farm on Monday, Tuesday and Wednesday. Ten-thirty till about one. Bring your lunch. Do you want to come? If you do, you have to come to all of them."

"Yes," answered Alice, firmly silencing her qualms and fears and the knowledge that Saffron wasn't ready to jump. "Yes, that's terrific. I'll be there."

Lizzie, who answered the Wheeler's telephone, said yes without even consulting the others.

"Well, I suppose it'll be all right," said Rupert when she told him. "David did say Rosie would be able to do cross-country with her peculiarly set-on head, and I suppose by some miracle she may discover how to take off."

Hanif was taken aback when Sarah told him that it was cross-country. "Are you sure he meant you to ask me?" he asked. "Because he told me that Jupiter wasn't ready to jump yet."

"You're definitely on the list," answered Sarah, checking. "Perhaps you don't have to do the jumps. I don't know, you'll just have to make up your mind."

"Well," said Hanif doubtfully. "I suppose you'd better include me in."

On Monday morning Alice and Hanif met in the lane outside Shawbury. They had crossed the river and the Waterford road and were trotting up the bridle path to Four Cross, when they saw Lesley Rooke coming from the direction of Woodbury. They waited for her at the crossroads.

"Hullo," they said. And Alice asked, "Isn't your sister coming?"

"She's gone on ahead with Tina Spencer. Mummy thought Tina might be useful putting up jumps."

"It was good of your sister to telephone everyone," said Hanif.

"Oh yes, well the Great Sarah has such a perfect telephone manner no one else can touch her," sneered Lesley.

Embarrassed by the viciousness in her voice, Hanif and Alice were pleased to see James waiting for them at the fruit farm gate.

"Jennifer's not coming," he told them gloomily. "She says it's pointless to train if David's not going to let us enter for the Cup and next year she'll be too old. She's right, of course. It's pointless for me too. I'll be fourteen next March, but my mother nagged me into coming. She has this idea you must have an interest; she even groomed Ferdie for me this morning. My sister Nina's potty about ballet so she's all right, but I'm not potty about anything."

"But you're a good rider and Ferdie's so lovely," said Alice, shocked. James's heavy, solemn face brightened at the compliment. "We never do anything new," he complained," and pottering over cavaletti for ever isn't much fun. I might enjoy it if we jumped something decent for a change—hedges and banks and streams."

"Do you think we will?" asked Hanif in horror.

"No, not in this pony club," answered James.

"You can't expect people to give up the time to make grand jumps," Lesley told him briskly. "The Cranford Vale raised a lot of money from a barbecue to pay for their cross-country course and they've got two or three keen fathers who built it. There aren't enough of us to hold a barbecue and none of the parents take much interest."

Alice and Hanif both had nervous flutterings and gnawing sensations in their stomachs as they rode up the Garland Farm lane, and the sight of Mr Roberts, helped by Paul and Lynne, loading poles, drums, and flags into the Land Rover did nothing to calm them.

James groaned loudly. "I knew it. I wish I'd taken Jennifer's advice. It's going to be the same old scene."

"Except that it's all going to Coppice Hill," Paul told him.

"Look at Chess. Isn't he beautiful?" Sarah appeared from the cattle yard leading Chess, his white parts showing pink skin through the damp hair, his mane half plaited. "We've been practising for the turnout."

"*You* won't do any good in that," said Lesley scathingly. "Your tack's too old and you're hopeless at plaiting."

"Lynne's teaching me to plait and I'll persuade Mummy to buy me some new tack before next Easter," Sarah snapped back.

"Tina can go in the Land Rover with David and steady these poles," decided Paul.

"I'd rather bike along with the rest of you," said Tina, feeling suddenly shy.

"You can't bike along the track to Coppice Hill. It's deep mud. The tractors have been churning it up all winter and we drove the cattle along it last week when we put them out on the hills."

"Tina can ride Berry and I'll go with David," offered Lynne. "I can ride round the farm any day."

"Oh thanks," Tina's thin, freckled face lit up. "Are you sure?"

"David said we were to start and he'd catch up with us, but the Wheelers aren't here yet," complained Paul.

"If they've any sense they'll go straight to Coppice Hill." Lynne told him. "It's much nearer for them to go along the sunken lane from Kidlake, but if they turn up here I'll send them on."

Paul mounted and led the way along the muddy track, the single wire of an electric fence separating them from the pale green of young oats. Saffron and Jupiter jogged impatiently on Banjo's tail. Lesley rode with James, but they didn't speak to each other, and behind them, Sarah shrieked with annoyance as Chess's immaculately white patches were splashed with liquid mud.

Netti and Lizzie were waiting in the sunken lane.

"We've lost Rupert."

"He forgot his lunch so he went back for it, ages ago," they explained.

"He'll turn up," said James.

"But he's so vague," Lizzie looked down the lane with a worried expression. "I think I'd better go and look for him."

"Oh, don't be pathetic," snapped Lesley. "He can't possibly lose himself between Kidlake and here."

"You don't know Rupert." Netti giggled. "He's probably half-way to the Woodbury Riding School by now, I don't suppose he listened when we told him we were going to Coppice Hill."

"Here's the Land Rover," said Paul, dismounting and tugging at the slip rails that led from the lane into the rough pasture at the foot of the hill. "Get out of the way, Tina. David will want to drive in."

"Morning all," said David, opening the Land Rover door to inspect the nine riders and ponies. "Who's missing, Rupert?"

"Yes, he forgot his lunch."

"Well, we're going to begin by schooling, so perhaps some of you could mark out a school with the smaller drums. The flattest place you can find. Along the hedge, I should think."

"The short sides will be up and down hill," complained Paul.

"Only slightly. It won't matter for the sort of schooling we're going to do."

James, groaning at the prospect of more schooling, insisted on pacing out the distances and the correct placing of the oil drums. Hanif, delighted at even a temporary reprieve from the horrors of the hill, helped him willingly. As they remounted, a mud-bespattered Rupert came galloping up the track.

"Sorry," he said, dropping his rucksack beside the others. "I went up to the farm by mistake."

"Well, now you're all here, form up the ride and start walking round the school," said David. "Then I'll tell you what we're going to do."

James took the lead and the others followed him, grading themselves according to size. David settled himself on his shooting stick, and Tina, who'd given Berry back to Lynne, perched herself on the front bumper of the Land Rover and waited to see if she was needed.

"I decided on a cross-country course—it's going to be a sort of introduction to cross-country riding—" said David, "because most of your ponies aren't ready for show-jumping, which requires a fairly high degree of schooling. Cross-country, riding up and down hill and over rough going, popping over natural fences, is good for young horses. It muscles them up and improves their balance. Because you have plenty of space you don't have to ask for instant obedience and you don't need collection, or at least not until the fences become large and complicated. By choosing cross-country, I reckon we can improve every one of these ponies far more than if we had stayed in the paddock, schooling and jumping on the flat. Any questions?"

"Why do we have to school? Why not get going with the cross-country right away?" asked James.

"Because I have to make sure that you're all riding properly and that the ponies are going well. It's no fun riding an out-of-control pony downhill, so we've got to get them all going forward and on the bit before we begin. So, start riding forward now. I want to see them all over-tracking: that is, taking such a long energetic step with their hindlegs that the hoof comes down on or in front of the hoofprint left by the fore-foot." He paused and watched them.

"Rajah and Rosie aren't overtracking, nor is Stardust, nor Chess, nor Banjo. Three of you are jogging. Only Ferdinand and Tristram are walking properly. Come on— legs. One at a time. Try and feel the pony's stride and then fit your legs in to ask him for a longer step. We don't want a hurried walk, but we do want an energetic one."

When the lively ponies had been persuaded to settle down and everyone was overtracking in a determined manner, David told them to trot and they were soon circling and changing the rein and sepentining, with angry roars directed at those who let their ponies look the wrong way.

"It is tremendously important that a cross-country pony looks where he is going," said David when he had halted them for a rest. "I know that some of the show-jumpers look the wrong way on corners, but you'll generally find they're beaten by the ones who are correctly bent when it comes to jumping off against the clock. The trouble is that you all use your outside reins to hold the ponies out on corners and circles. You mustn't. You're *making* them look the wrong way."

"But if I don't, Ra just cuts in," protested Lizzie.

"So does Berry."

"All right, we'll try a new exercise. Divide into two rides. James leads the bigger ponies, Netti the small ones. James, your lot are to make a circle in the other half of the school, I don't want to be trampled on. The rest of you watch."

When they were all circling at the walk, David told them to make the circle gradually smaller using only their outside reins and legs. "That's the idea," he said. "All right, that's small enough. Now I want you to make it bigger, gradually, using only the inside rein and leg. No outside hands, just the inside aids. See if you can do it."

To their surprise all the riders found they could, that by turning the ponies heads inwards and using the inside leg they could make the circles large again. David propped himself against the Land Rover and had his two rides circling in the two halves of the school. They tried at the walk and trot and were soon all patting their ponies enthusiastically.

"Now we're going to canter," said David. "Not a school canter but a cross-country one. It's rather faster and freer. You sit forward, your weight in your stirrups and just above your saddle. You use the lower leg to keep the pony going with impulsion and on the bit. Your reins are shorter and

66

your arms more extended. Don't worry, it's quite easy," he added as some of the riders began to put themselves in strange positions. "Just pull up your stirrups a couple of holes, more if you ride very long, and we'll try it out at the trot."

"I shall probably end up in Woodbury," Hanif told Alice as they stopped to alter their stirrups. "See you tomorrow morning, same time."

"I'm going to turn Rosie uphill if she tries anything," decided Rupert.

"The trouble about that is you have to come down again," Hanif pointed out.

"I'll dismount and lead her," said Rupert.

David insisted on a very energetic trot. "Now that you're riding short you can't use your seats as a driving aid, and that's a disadvantage," he told them. "But you will be able to stay balanced and with your ponies up and down hill, over rough ground and over fences, which you can't do if you're riding long and sitting deep. It's a different sort of riding, but we still want the ponies full of impulsion and going on the bit. You've got to use what leg you've got left harder, but no kicking, Lesley."

When he had them all trotting round in a very energetic manner, he told them to stand in their stirrups and pretend they were riding at the cross-country canter.

"James, not as high as that. Sharpen the angles of your heels, knees and hips, then you'll come closer to the saddle."

"Lizzie, you're looking down, stiffening your elbows and resting your hands on the pony's neck. Your weight must be over your stirrups. No pony can jump with the rider's weight on his neck."

"Lesley, that's much better, but stop kicking. If she won't obey your legs, use your whip. If you kick you'll always have to kick. You've got to teach your pony to obey a proper leg aid."

"Stop messing about at the back. Sit closer to your saddles. Sharpen up those angles."

67

Lynne and Sarah were tipping about and giggling help-lessly as they tried to stand in their stirrups. Paul was crouched over Banjo's neck and looked as though he were riding the final stages of a flat race.

"Rising trot," ordered David. "Paul, you're going ahead of your pony. Straighten up your back and push him on ahead of you. This is something you could all think about," he shouted. "You should always have the feeling that two-thirds of your pony is in front of you and only one third behind. I'm sure that Paul, Lizzie, Rupert and Lesley feel the opposite. They've only got one third in front and two thirds trailing behind. But I want you all to try to recognise the feeling, because it's one way of telling if a pony is going well."

"Prepare to canter on. James, we want a brisk pace. Make the school bigger by going outside the drums and anyone who finds he's catching the horse in front, go wide and pass on the outside. Remember, sit forward and ride forward. Canter on."

Hanif had expected to be run away with at once, but, to his surprise, Jupiter seemed quite content with the pace that James had set. They thundered round the school with David shouting at Lizzie to look up, to study the trees or the sky, instead of always the ground. At Lesley to chase the pony in front of her. At several people to sharpen the angles of their heels, knees and hips, and at everyone to use his or her legs.

The ponies were beginning to puff, when he called to James to change the rein, trotting at X and starting off on the other leg. Several people got angry yells because they let their ponies stumble into the trot, or kicked them into a canter.

"We don't want messy transitions," roared David. "Ride them, you've got legs."

Soon they were all flying round on the other rein, chasing each other energetically. The ponies were glad when the order came to walk.

"All right," said David. "I think you've all got the idea.

68

You can have a rest. Get off the ponies and give their backs a rest too."

"That was great," said Rupert, patting Rosie's sweaty neck quite lovingly. "It's the best she's ever gone for me."

"I'm still here, I can't believe it," observed Hanif. "Oh Jupe, you were a marvel of good behaviour."

"Saffy went quite well too," said Alice. "I think he likes my cross-country seat, especially at the canter."

Then everyone began to complain about his or her aching legs, but they were very cheerful and even James's solemn face wore a smile, while Lesley unbent enough to tell Alice that Stardust was a lot faster than she had thought.

After a few minutes, David interrupted the chatter. "I was pleased with the riders of the bigger ponies," he said. "They were all working hard, but the four of you at the back weren't doing so well. As I've said before, just because you've got nice easy ponies you think you can sit there having an easy time, but you can't. You're still passive riders. You can walk, trot and canter and stop more or less when you want to, but you don't influence the *way* your pony walks, trots or canters. If you're going to be any good you must start using your legs and your brains." He eased himself off his shooting stick and stood up. "Now, we're going on to the next stage and I'll need some help with the flags."

"Ferdie doesn't mind flags, where do you want them put?" asked James.

"On the hillside in the next field. I'll drive through and show you. Can someone take down the slip rails, please?"

In the second field the hill rose much more steeply, and the flat space along the floor of the valley was narrower.

"He's not really going to make us go up there, is he?" asked Hanif, gazing up at the coppice on the crest and giving an apprehensive shudder.

"From the look of the flags, we've only got to go up half way," Rupert observed, as they watched James press two red flags on canes into the ground at points along the hillside, while Lizzie, who had lent Rajah to Tina to ride round, drove along the valley with David and put up two lower flags, opposite James's.

"Now," said David, when they had all gathered round the Land Rover, "it's fairly obvious what we're going to do. You start, one at a time, from here. Ride along the valley to the first flag, turn uphill, ride straight for the next flag halfway up, go outside it, no cutting of corners, turn left and carry on along the hillside towards number three, outside that, turn downhill and ride straight for number four where you halt. Then you *walk* back here. The rest of the time you ride at a steady trot, and I mean a *steady trot*. We all know what the ponies will want to do, they'll dawdle uphill, hurry downhill, cut the corners and charge back here to their friends. But the riders are to be in charge, not the ponies. Any questions?"

"Supposing you can't keep the same steady trot?" asked Hanif.

"You can, if you use your legs," answered David. "Ride well forward in the saddle uphill, if you keep your weight off your pony's loins you make it easier for him. Keep him going nicely along the top and use your legs like hell coming down. If you're having difficulty in keeping the pony's hindlegs under him, you can sit close to the saddle and use your seat too, but don't start leaning back or hanging on to the reins or you'll give yourself a rough time. You come down riding the pony forward and sitting with the jumping seat, so that when we start *jumping* downhill there'll be no problems."

"Do we really have to trot coming down?" asked Lesley.

"Yes."

"Supposing we simply *can't* stop?" inquired Hanif.

"You'll have to circle, but make up your mind that you're going to ride forward and use your legs and you *will* stop. Right, we'll change the order of the ride for this. James first, then Lizzie, Netti, Paul, Rupert, Sarah, Alice, Lesley, Lynne and finally Harry."

"Would it be O.K. if I loaned Tristram to Tina and he went twice? He's quite fit," asked Netti.

70

"No. I'm not worried about the pony, but I can't have Tina riding up and downhill when I haven't seen her in the school. If anyone can lend her a pony tomorrow, she can join in the schooling and we'll see how she goes."

"Ollie might lend Hobbit," suggested Lizzie. "He's a bit small, but Tina's very light."

"You'd have to bribe him," said Rupert.

"He might agree if we said he could help David with the jumps."

"It's a brilliant idea. I'll persuade him," Netti told Tina, as James set off along the valley at the steadiest of trots. Soon Ferdie, confronted by the hill began to slow down, but David produced a loudhailer and the valley echoed with his cries of 'legs!'. Horse and rider made an elegant pair as they crossed the hillside, but they slowed to a very cautious trot as they turned downhill.

"Legs! Keep him going. Look up!" David was shouting as they came down and halted just past the flag.

"All right, not bad," was his verdict.

"Not bad! I thought it was brilliant," said Sarah.

"It was the first time I've trotted down a hill as steep as that," said James, patting Ferdinand and looking quite pleased with himself.

The others were watching Lizzie. She had had to work hard to keep Rajah trotting up the hill, but she was going well along the top. David told Netti to start and, as the little grey tackled the uphill, Lizzie and Rajah turned round the third flag and came to a dead halt, both peering at the slope before them with horrified expressions.

"Legs, I said keep trotting!" roared David. "Look up! Get going!"

Lizzie urged Rajah into a reluctant trot, but his wise chestnut face wore a very disapproving expression as he slid thankfully to a halt beside the final flag.

"Not bad for the first time," said David, signalling to Paul to start. Netti was enjoying herself as she turned downhill. She used her legs feverishly and felt Tristram's hindlegs go further under him. He stayed balanced and halted close to the flag.

"Good," said David.

"It was lovely," Netti told the others. "Using the legs really worked. Only now they feel ready to drop off."

Paul was much less controlled. As he came round the third flag Banjo broke into a canter. He hauled him hastily back to a walk. Then he got him trotting, but missed the flag and halted almost in the hedge.

"Rotten," shouted David. "You see, you're not in control."

Rosie had left the other ponies reluctantly and weaved an uncertain path along the valley. The uphill was an effort for her. She began by cantering and then slowed to a puffing walk.

"Legs!" yelled David.

Rupert got her going along the hillside, but when she saw the downhill slope she came to an abrupt halt. Urged on by Rupert's legs and David's yells, she was persuaded to slip and slither down at a sprawling trot. Then she saw the other ponies and decided on a short cut, charging back to them at a canter, with a surprised Rupert pulling ineffectually on the reins.

"Take her straight back to the top flag," ordered David. "And this time be ready for her—right rein and left leg—and halt beside the final flag."

As Rosie came down for the second time and halted only a few yards from the flag, Sarah appeared at the top of the slope.

"Come on, faster. Why are you walking?" roared David as Chess picked his way down cautiously. "Legs!"

Saffron had started well, but, coming along the hillside, the feel of great open spaces seemed to go to his head. He trotted faster and faster and when Alice tried to control him he began stargazing. They came round the third flag, broke into a canter, whirled past Chess, and Saffron, ignoring Alice's attempts to make him circle, careered into the group of waiting ponies. With a furious squeal, Berry lashed out at him. One of her hoofs thudded against his chest.

David swore. "Is he all right? Bring him over here and let me see."

Alice had dismounted.

"His chest's a bit cut, but it doesn't look very deep," she answered as she led Saffron over.

"Paul, could you get the first aid kit from the Land Rover?" asked David as he inspected the wound. "Better give it a quick bathe and a puff or two of wound powder. Has the pony had a permanent anti-tet?"

"I don't know," answered Alice, taking the bathing bowl from Paul.

"Well you *must* find out, and quickly. Telephone his owner the moment you get home and, if he hasn't had a permanent one, the vet will have to come out and give him the ordinary one. It has to be done today because tetanus is a killer and, as I expect you all know, it's in the earth, so a kick with a muddy hoof can easily transmit the germ. And it doesn't need a serious wound, any little cut or scratch will do. That's why it's important that all your ponies should have the permanent anti-tet with boosters as necessary, and so should all of you. Right, Sarah, get back up that hill and come down at a *trot*. You're the boss, not the pony."

Lesley had stopped and waited when she saw the confusion ahead, but as Sarah rode uphill for her second attempt, she came round the red flag and began to walk down. Despite David's ferocious roars she made no attempt to trot, and, when she halted neatly at the final flag, he said, "Straight back, and this time trot. And look ahead, not down at the ground."

Chess was still disapproving, but slightly less cautious at his second attempt. Lesley came down at a grudging tight-reined trot. Then it was Alice. Saffron seemed none the worse for his kick.

"Now get him on the bit before you come round the flag. You've got a difficult pony so I don't mind if you stop or circle. Get him on the bit and ride forward. If you don't keep pushing him on you'll lose him. I know it sounds silly but it's the truth."

Alice, determined not to be galloped back to the other ponies, took a firm hold on her right rein with the result that Saffron began to come down sideways, almost at the full pass.

"Ride straight," roared David. "It's dangerous to come down sideways. He could cross his legs and fall. Use your legs and keep him straight."

Alice straightened him hastily and Saffron immediately broke into a canter and swept down the hill, but this time Alice managed to circle away to the right.

"Take him back and this time come down at the walk," shouted David.

Lynne had appeared. She came down the hill at a trot, but it became faster and faster as Berry lost her balance. As the trot became a canter Lynne's crash cap flew off and she was laughing and giving excited shrieks as they whirled round and stopped dead among the other ponies.

"Very bad. You didn't even attempt to use your legs," said David. "Take her back and come down properly."

Hanif had set off steadily, and the steepness of the uphill had kept Jupiter going at a sober pace, but along the top he had increased his speed despite endless half-halts, Hanif knew he was losing control and viewed the flag ahead with feelings of impending doom. "Steady boy. Whoa, Jupe, steady," he said as he turned the corner. Jupiter saw the other ponies and Hanif the full horror of the slope.

"Half-halt, legs," roared David as Jupiter broke into a canter, but Hanif felt as though his legs were made of some soft substance, cotton wool, he thought, as Jupiter snatched the reins from him and thundered down the hill.

"Circle," shouted David.

Hanif tried. Right rein, left leg, he told himself. He must at least prevent Jupe from galloping into the other ponies and getting kicked. With Jupiter fighting to turn left and Hanif struggling to turn him to the right, they stayed on a straight course, racing towards the thick, overgrown hedge

74

which fenced the field from the lane. At the very last moment they pony realized he had to stop. He threw back his weight, his hoofs skidded, Hanif shot over his head and landed in a thicket of thorn and bramble.

"Are you all right?" asked David.

Rupert went after Jupiter, who trotted away, reins dangling. Alice hurried to the hedge.

"Are you hurt, Harry?"

"No, I don't think so. Just spiked and pierced," answered Hanif, trying to disentangle himself from clutching brambles as he emerged backwards from the hedge.

"Your face is bleeding."

"Where?"

Alice pointed and Hanif dabbed at his cheek with his handkerchief. "It's not much," he said, inspecting the blood, "and I've no beauty to lose."

"One disgracefully bad pony." Rupert appeared towing Jupiter from Rosie.

"It was lack of legs," said David. "You stopped using them when you saw the hill. You should have made a half-halt and used your legs in the interest of self-preservation. Up you go again and keep his hindlegs under him."

Hanif trotted up the hill feeling heavy-hearted and weak-legged. He knew he couldn't do it and, sure enough, Jupiter was off the moment he pointed him downhill, only this time he agreed to circle and they avoided crashing into the hedge.

"All right, you wait here a minute. I want to send the others round again. Are you ready, James? Same steady trot. Unless there's a hold-up, you all start when the pony ahead of you is halfway up the hill. Alice, you'd better walk down."

Nearly everyone was much better at the second attempt.

Alice, who walked halfway down and then lost control when she tried a trot, was sent back. But Lynne, who again whirled down giving squeaks of excitement, got an angry roar of, "You're not trying."

"James, you take Harry's pony, and Lizzie, let's see you

on Berry. And, while they're sorting themselves out, the rest of you can go round again. Alice, you lead."

The ponies were settling down. They were no longer excited by the feeling of space. They set off soberly, and soon the hillside was covered in ponies all moving at the same steady trot and not attempting to overtake each other.

"Good," David was shouting. "Well done. That was much better," as rider after rider came down the hill and halted at the flag.

James and Lizzie had had a ride along the valley to try out their strange mounts.

"He's strong and very gassy," James told David.

"Berry's got terribly rough paces," complained Lizzie.

"Yes, she's a real old-fashioned harness pony," agreed David. "She really picks her feet up and you see an awful lot of her knees. It's not the right action for a riding pony, but that doesn't mean she has to run away downhill. Are you two ready? Off you go then and all the others can follow."

Hanif watched James carefully. He was older, stronger and more experienced, so he didn't mind learning from him, and he felt pleased to see how well Jupiter was going. David was roaring "Legs!" and "Half-halt!" at intervals. When they turned downhill, Jupiter made a determined effort to take control but when he did begin to canter, James turned him uphill again and took him back to the flag. Suddenly Jupiter gave in and decided to behave. He trotted down smoothly and made a very elegant halt.

"Terrific," said David.

"He's not easy." James rode over, patting Jupiter. "Shall I take him round again? Would Harry like to try Ferdie? He's much easier."

"He's a bit big for Harry," said David, watching Berry. "Well done, Lizzie, but do remember to look up when you halt. I know, we'll try Harry on Stardust. I'd like to see her with another rider. The rest of you keep going round."

76

They were nearly all delighted to go round again. They had decided that they enjoyed riding downhill. Only Hanif, using his legs frantically to keep Stardust going, almost wished himself back on Jupiter. But he managed to keep her trotting down the hill and to halt at the flag, while Jupiter, who had stopped rolling his eyes and arguing, was pretending to be an obedient and well-schooled pony.

"Back on your own nags," said David, "and everyone but Lynne and Harry can ride the course the other way round. You will halt at the far flag and then *walk* back here. Anyone who comes charging back out of control will be expelled from the course."

"But that hill's steeper."

"Much steeper," they began to complain, looking at the slope suspiciously.

"Yes, it is a bit, but now you've learned to ride downhill you can ride down *any* hill. You don't have to start measuring gradients. Plenty of leg, look where you're going and halt at the flag. Lead on, James."

Some people crept down the distant hill, some went too fast, but they all managed it, and the second time round it began to seem easy. Alice had discovered that if she began by walking she could then push Saffron forward into a trot when she had him going well and this worked much better than beginning fast and losing control.

Then it was Hanif's and Lynne's turn. They both set off with very determined expressions on their faces. Hanif was in the lead and he felt much more confident than before. He knew now that he could do the hill and Jupiter could do it. It's just a matter of legs, he told himself, gritting his teeth as he fought to keep Jupiter balanced. It worked. He didn't halt absolutely at the flag, but he halted.

"Well done," shouted David. "Go round once more."

Lynne, rather indignant that Lizzie had controlled her pony so easily, concentrated this time and found that she too could make Berry behave if she tried. She felt quite pleased with herself as she followed Hanif round for another try.

When they came back they found the other pony club members all dismounted and gossiping.

"That's all for today," said David. "Tomorrow morning, here at the same time."

"Thank you very much," they said.

"Yes, it was terrific."

"Great."

"The best rally ever."

"Except for the inconvenience of damaged legs," said Rupert. "Mine have never ached so much in my life."

"It's the first time in your life that you've used them," retorted David, twisting himself into the Land Rover.

"Would you like Banjo, Tina?" asked Paul. "I'll go with David and do the slip rails."

The ponies were weary and were quite happy to walk back to the farm on a loose reins while their riders discussed the morning.

"It was far more fun than an ordinary rally," said James, "and we actually learned something new."

"The ponies enjoyed it, which was nice," remarked Lizzie. "At least I'm sure Ra prefers cross-country to ordinary schooling. David says he's to have a worm dose and then I'm to increase his oats and nuts. Do you think Mummy'll have a fit at the expense?"

"Two, probably," said Rupert.

"No, she won't," argued Netti. "She oughtn't to anyway. Parents are always wanting you to take things seriously, so now we're doing it they ought to be pleased and take notice of what David says."

"I've been giving Stardust huge feeds since last Wednesday," Lesley told Lizzie. "I think it's beginning to have an effect. She wouldn't have trotted up that hill in the Christmas holidays."

When James saw all the other pony club members watering their ponies and tying them up with feeds, before settling down to eat their own lunches in one of the empty barns, he felt rather sad that he couldn't stay.

"I'll bring mine tomorrow," he said, waving goodbye as he rode away down the lane.

"Tina, will you come home with us and try Hobbit?" asked Lizzie. "We've decided to tell Ollie that it'll be a huge advantage to have a ready-schooled cross-country pony next year, when he's old enough to go on the course."

"I'd love to try him," answered Tina, "but I have a feeling David will take one look at me and say I'm not good enough."

"You know, it's very odd," said Hanif, sitting down on Alice's straw bale. "If you have bikes or cars you can give one set of instructions to *all* the owners, but with ponies that wouldn't work at all. David looks round and says that this one mustn't wear a pelham, but that one can. Some need dropped nosebands and others don't. Jupe mustn't have oats, Rajah and Stardust must have more. Even the riding instructions are different for different people."

"Except for legs," said Alice ruefully. "We *all* get yelled at to use them."

"It does seem to work though," observed Tina. "I've watched Mr Foster and all the working pupils teaching at the riding school. They don't get as excited as David. They go on and on about heels down and straight backs and hands low, but nothing ever seems to change. I learned a lot watching today because when the riders did the right thing the ponies *did* change. It was quite exciting."

"You wait till you're at the receiving end of David's roars," Rupert told her, "you won't find it so exciting then. Does anyone know what happens to overworked legs? Do they wither away?"

"No, of course not," Lesley sounded cross at such absurdity. "If you use muscles, they develop. They wither when you *don't* use them."

"You mean we're all going to end up with huge thick legs, really brawny ones, like blacksmiths' arms?"

"No, she doesn't. Don't tease," Lizzie told her brother.

"The Cranford Vale people all have quite nice legs," said Sarah, inspecting her own, "and they must use them or they wouldn't win everything."

79

The Robertses came into the barn to ask if Tina had put Banjo away in the cattle yard and found his water and feed.

"Yes, everything was fine," answered Tina, "and he drank two buckets of water."

"I asked David if he'd like us to start building the cross-country course this afternoon," Paul went on, his face serious, "but he said he was too whacked to think about tomorrow. I don't know how we're ever going to get those jumps built."

"I hope we haven't tired him out too much," said Lizzie, looking anxious.

"Mum says it's good for him to have an interest, and we won't do him any harm so long as we don't ride over him," Lynne told her in comfortable tones.

CHAPTER FIVE

We'll Never Do It

Except for Tina, all the pony club members were much more confidant and light-hearted when they rode to Garland Farm on the second morning of the course. Tina had tried Hobbit out on Monday afternoon and liked him very much. He was a little, dark brown Dartmoor, handy and willing, who raced round the Wheelers' messy jumps with ease.

"He's lovely," Tina had said, patting him afterwards with a smile on her thin freckled face. "It's very kind of Ollie to lend him to me, and of you to arrange everything."

"He only has two faults," Lizzie answered. "One is that he hates cantering on the near fore—Ollie can never get him on it—and the other is that he didn't grow when we did. It was so lovely when Rupert had Tristram and Hobbit was mine. We felt that we were quite good riders, and we did fairly well at the pony club, but now, with Rosie and Ra, we feel right out of everything. We used to be the equals of James and Jennifer when they had their little ponies, but now we're not in the same class at all."

"Of course, if you've *never* had a pony of your own, you long to have one so much you don't really care how hopeless it is," Tina had said, as she unbuckled Hobbit's cardboard-stiff bridle and threw his green encrusted bit in the bucket of water, "but I suppose once you've had a good one you feel differently."

"Yes, I do love Ra, but I can't help feeling envious when I see everyone else whirling over jumps so easily, and Rupert minds even more," Lizzie had agreed sadly.

When Tina arrived back at Kidlake at nine the next morning, Oliver was grooming Hobbit unwillingly.

"Thank goodness," he said, handing her his dandy

81

brush, "I thought you were never coming. I've picked out his hoofs and groomed a quarter of him."

"Which quarter?" asked Tina, looking from Oliver's round, cheeky face to the mud-caked pony.

"Near fore," answered Oliver. "The front is much nicer to groom than the back, except for the head. I hate grooming heads, they're all corners."

"He's the laziest boy on earth," said Lizzie, who was dodging Rajah's angry nips as she groomed his stomach.

Tina had taken off her anorak and was brushing energetically. She was used to grooming dozens of ponies to earn one ride at Mr Foster's. It was a real treat to be getting one ready for herself, she thought.

"Well, you *must* help David with the jumps and flags and things," Netti told Oliver in an elder-sisterly voice. "If you start being silly or showing-off we won't take you again."

"I might not want to go again," countered Oliver. "And I might come home if it's boring."

"Has anyone seen my bridle?" demanded Rupert, appearing dramatically at the back door. "It's completely vanished. I've looked everywhere, and now I'm going to be late again and this time David will be furious."

"It's probably hanging up in the tackroom. You know how hopeless you are at looking," Netti told him.

Lizzie stopped grooming and stood with an anxious expression on her face, trying to cast her mind back to the evening before.

"You cleaned it while you were watching television, don't you remember? Mummy was cross when you spilled metal polish on the rug."

"Yes, but where is it *now*?"

"Rupert and Rosie are both a bit dozey, Ra and Liz are both in a tiz," chanted Oliver.

The Rookes' separate arrangements didn't go according to plan. Lesley had made her way to the field early, cleaned her tack as Stardust munched her way contentedly through her extra large feed, and then started grooming. But Sarah, who had cleaned her tack at home the night before, persuaded her mother to drive her to the field and, grooming briskly, found herself ready to start at the same moment as her sister.

"Aren't you waiting for Tina?" asked Lesley as they approached the gate together.

"Of course not. You *know* she's borrowing Hobbit from the Wheelers. She's gone over to Kidlake to groom him."

"I can't remember every little detail about what your friends are doing," snapped Lesley.

"Who cares," said Sarah, fastening the gate. "By the way, Mum's coming to watch tomorrow. She's going to leave Janet and Mrs Cox in charge of the Ds and come to Coppice Hill."

"That'll ruin everything." Lesley's voice was bitter with anger. "She'll interfere. She'll keep telling David what a wonderful little rider The Great Sarah is and how he should put *her* on all the sticky ponies."

"She won't. Why are you always so horrible, so cross and jealous?"

"Because I'm sick and tired of hearing your praises all day. Because you're Mummy's nasty, slimy little pet," shouted Lesley, her anger getting the better of her.

"It's not my fault. I can't help it. I didn't *ask* to be Mum's favourite," Sarah shouted back.

They rode on in angry silence. Sarah took a sideways glance at her sister's face and thought, it's no wonder Mum likes me best when she's so ugly and cross and boring; it's her own fault.

Lesley escaped from her seething indignation into a dream world. She began to imagine a great triumph. Sarah had made a complete mess of the cross-country jumps, then it was her turn. She rode brilliantly, whirling downhill, clearing everything. "Well done," shouted David through the loudhailer, then he turned to her mother and added, "That's the horsewoman of your family, Mrs Rooke."

Sarah took another look at her sister. Oh let her sulk, she thought. I don't care. Soon I'll be with Lynne and Netti and

Tina and I like them a million times better than Lesley.

Alice and Hanif had ridden over to Garland Farm with short stirrups and their cross-country seats. They arrived with aching legs, but a feeling of accomplishment for there was do doubt that their ponies went better when ridden in this manner. Saffron hadn't stargazed, Jupiter hadn't pulled and they had both gone with pricked ears and contented expressions.

David was already in the yard, leaning against the Land Rover. He had spread a large sheet of paper on the bonnet and seemed to be going through details of a plan with Mr Roberts.

"What about the anti-tet?" he asked Alice.

"It was O.K.. I rang Mr Crankshaw and he'd been done."

"Good. Bring him over here and let me have a look at the wound. Oh yes, that's healing nicely. Now do keep away from Berry, all of you, she's in a very mare-ish mood. If everybody's here, you can go on, I'll follow in a minute or two."

"He really is planning a cross-country course, isn't he?" James asked Paul as they set off along the farm track.

"Yes, we're to help Dad with the jumps after lunch," answered Paul, "but I don't think they're going to be much—mostly baling string and poles, though they have looked out a plastic sheet for the water."

"Water? To jump?" asked Hanif in horrified tones.

"Yes, and a ditch."

"Chess can't bear black plastic," moaned Sarah. "He's got a phobia. When we went as a junior team to the Cranford Vale hunter trials he refused three times. Afterwards Mum got all sorts of people to try to get him over, but they couldn't; he just won't go near it. It's a phobia, everyone said so."

"David will know what to do." Alice tried to comfort them. "After all, we couldn't ride downhill until he told us how."

"I'm not at all sure I can do it today," observed Hanif gloomily. "Yesterday might have been a fluke, or just that Jupe was too worn out to keep up the argument."

84

The Wheelers and Tina came trotting along the lane from Kidlake at the same moment as the Land Rover appeared, and James and Paul dismounted to take down the slip rails.

"Will you put them up again when I'm through?" asked David. "Drop the top rail at the right-hand end. I want you all to jump in over them. Don't make a great fuss about it, just pop over. James first, large and lively ponies in the front, and Lynne, keep Berry well away from everyone. All right?"

He drove through and waited. The riders milled about in the lane, arguing.

"Give me some room, I want a run," demanded James.

Oliver who had appeared on a bicycle, flung it in the hedge and asked what was going on.

Ferdie popped over neatly, Jupiter shot after him, hurled himself over and set off at a gallop across the field, but finding that Ferdie was standing calmly by the Land Rover and that Hanif had turned him uphill, he slowed down. Saffron charged over, head in air. Rosie refused dead, her nose almost touching the ground on the far side.

"Go back and take another lead," shouted David, clearing the way for Rajah who came over in slow motion. Stardust trotted up and refused. Tristram passed her and flew over. Banjo took it neatly and was followed by Chess, Hobbit and Berry. Rosie refused again and so did Stardust, with a disappointed Lesley kicking frantically.

"Hold it," David shouted to them. "Alice and Harry, you jump back into the lane and give them a lead. Lesley," he went on, grabbing the loudhailer, "don't *kick*. Use your whip to get the pony going before you start jumping, then sit still and use your legs properly—invisibly. Nothing could jump with you throwing yourself about like that."

Oliver, who had used the lull in the jumping to come through, approached David. "I'm supposed to be helping you," he said.

"Great, I need it. As soon as those two ponies have jumped back will you see if you can find a pole or branch to act as a ground line. Put it about two feet in front of the slip rail. Rosie wants some help in finding her take-off."

Hanif was looking at the slip rails doubtfully. There was a grass verge to land on and then the lane. It was all slightly downhill. "Go on, don't make a great thing about it. Just pop over," David shouted to him.

Jupiter made an unnecessarily large jump, but, as there was no where to gallop to, he stopped of his own accord. Alice trotted and popped without any stargazing this time. They decided that Hanif should give Rupert a lead and Alice, Lesley. The two girls went back a long way down the lane to give Lesley a chance to get Stardust going.

"Wait, wait! you've got to have a ground line," Oliver was shouting at his brother. With loud crackings and splinterings he pulled a rotten branch off a tree and dragged it along the lane.

"Will this do?" he shouted at David.

"Yes, fine. A good two feet in front."

Hanif turned Jupiter at the fence and bounded over, but Rosie did another of her head-down refusals.

"Follow the girls," shouted David, as Alice and Lesley came cantering up the lane and both flew over easily. Rosie refused again.

"Right, on to the school, all of you. She won't like it when she finds she's on her own," said David. "Come on, Oliver, leave her."

Rosie neighed indignantly as they all jogged on across the field, and then, deciding that she would have to jump, she heaved herself over from a standstill and galloped after the other ponies, giving a series of unseating-looking bucks. Rupert arrived at the school laughing.

"I don't know how you stayed on," said Alice. "It looked horrible."

"He's got such long legs he never falls off," Oliver told her.

"He's like the sugar tongs in the poem," added Netti. "'His legs are so long and so aptly constructed': It's a great help."

86

"Form up the ride, the same order as yesterday," said David. "And we want everyone riding with long stirrups, please. Do remember that you now have two distinct seats —and keep them distinct. Whatever you do, don't ride short unless you're sitting forward. Sitting at the back of the saddle with short stirrups is always a disaster. You can't influence the pony's hindlegs and your weight is too far back, you're behind the pony's movement.

"Lynne, you'd better go last, we don't want Tina's pony kicked. Now, an energetic walk. Make sure they're over-tracking."

They walked and trotted and circled. They made circles larger and smaller. Except for Rosie, they leg-yielded then they serpentined with encouraging shouts from David, who said that they were all getting the idea at last. There were groans when everyone but Lynne had to cross their stirrups, and they practised halting from the trot. Rosie and Saffron were allowed to make very slow transitions through the walks but the others were expected to manage with only two or three steps of walking.

"Sit up. Take your weight back a little. Sit deep. Use your legs," roared David. "Go on riding forward until you've actually halted. We want their hindlegs under them, not trailing behind. They must stand at attention, not straggle all over the place."

Everyone was relieved when they were told to have a rest and shorten their stirrups for cantering.

"Do you think legs *ever* get used to it?" asked Rupert, flexing his ruefully when the cantering was over.

"At least with two seats you spread the aches," observed Alice. "Knees upwards for schooling and knees downwards for cross-country."

"Are you all right, Tina?" asked Lizzie. "It's a bit hard on you. We've worked up to this stage gradually."

"I'm fine. I do a lot of bareback riding, taking the ponies back to their fields, and Hobbit's lovely and easy to ride."

"Right, now I'm going on into the next field and Oliver's going to put the slip rails up again for you to jump in," said

David. "*Don't* ride on each other's tails. *Don't* get excited and *do* sit still. I'd rather see the odd stop, the occasional refusal, than people riding like maniacs at tiny jumps. Ponies don't need to be 'got over', they're quite capable of jumping small fences. Your job is to organize the correct pace, have the pony balanced and on the bit and, if you've walked the course and know what sort of fence lies ahead, indicate that knowledge to him. But if you're waving you're arms and legs about, you can't indicate anything, and the pony can't concentrate on jumping if you're giving him thumping great kicks in the ribs. So don't be a hindrance. Sit still and help."

Oliver was very efficient with the slip rails and even found an old broken rail to act as a ground line for Rosie. As soon as he shouted that it was ready, James set off at a steady canter and flew over the high end. Hanif and Alice jumped in the middle, Rupert rode at the low end and everyone cheered when Rosie jumped. The ponies seemed to be inspirng each other. Tristram and Stardust took it fast and sailed over and all the little ponies followed in fine style.

"Now we're going to do the hill the easy way, at the trot, twice," said David. "Off you go James. And as soon as one pony is half way up the hill the next one can start."

For most people the downhill had suddenly become easy; only Hanif, Alice, Rupert and Lynne still had to work hard to keep their ponies under control. Tina went down very cautiously the first time, but at her second attempt she managed to keep trotting and David sent her round a third time on her own.

Then they went round the other way. Alice and Hanif hadn't tried the steep hill before, but as everyone else could do it they were filled with a grim determination not to be beaten, and since their ponies, who were enjoying themselves, had become far more cooperative, they managed it quite easily.

"Good. Well done, everyone, especially Tina," said David when they had all been round twice. "Now I want

88

you to go the easy way at the canter. You all know what to do. Ride forward. Legs. Look where you're going and halt at the flag." ..

"Doesn't James look brilliant," said Netti as horse and rider crossed the hillside. "He looks like a competitor at Badminton."

"Very competent," agreed Rupert. "Harry doesn't look too bad either."

"They all look better at the canter," agreed Tina as Alice reached the second flag.

"I am about to spoil the pretty picture," said Rupert, turning Rosie and setting off in pursuit of Rajah.

The ponies were used to the hillside and the feeling of open spaces and they knew the routine so they were content to canter in order. They didn't attempt to overtake or race, and one by one the riders came back smiling and patting their mounts.

David had arranged for James and Alice to go with him in the Land Rover, and the moment Lynne and Berry returned he announced that the riders should dismount to give the ponies' backs a rest while he organized the jumps. He drove up the hill slantwise and stopped at mid-point between each pair of flags to deposit drums and poles. Soon there were three jumps, low ones with drums on their sides on the two hills and a larger one midway along the top. Rupert was relieved to see that they all had ground lines and everyone, even the boldest among them, was pleased to see that the downhill jump was so small.

"Right," said David, when everyone had remounted and Oliver, who was being very attentive, had handed him the loudhailer. "Now we're going to include the jumps this time and, once again, don't fuss. Start at the canter, get your weight well forward for the uphill jump, canter along the top and don't forget to use the half-halt to draw your pony's attention to the fact that there is now a jump there. He doesn't know. When you come to the third flag, slow up to a trot, then ride the pony forward over the jump. I don't mind whether you trot or canter the last bit, provided you halt at the flat. Any questions?"

"Must we trot at the third flag?" asked James.

"It depends on how effective your half-halts are," answered David. "The important thing is that your pony must be balanced and under control so that you can be pushing him *forward* as you come to the fence. If you're hanging on to his head and trying to slow him up he can't jump. Most of the ponies here would need to trot a couple of strides and then push on."

"If we give them their heads over the jump they can race off the moment they land," objected Lesley. "I don't see how we're supposed to keep control."

"You don't 'give them their heads', or at least you shouldn't once you've passed the beginner stage of jumping. You've all got firm seats, you can jump, now you're expected to learn how to jump well and how to be active riders and *help* your ponies. I've explained about approaching with impulsion, sitting still, using your legs quietly so that you don't disturb him. Now your hands should 'follow him'. That is, you keep a light contact with the pony's mouth and as he extends his neck over the fence you keep that contact but give him the freedom he needs by extending your arms, slowly, and with quiet movement of the elbows. Then, as he lands, your elbows slide back and you still have contact. But of course it isn't the reins which keep him balanced, it's your legs and seat which will do the hard work. All right, James, off you go."

James made it look easy, and Hanif, who had set off with a very anxious expression, managed to persuade Jupiter to trot to within three strides of the jump, then he cantered, but remained more or less in control and managed to halt a couple of yards from the flag. Alice brought Saffron to a walk at the third flag and then pushed him forward as they approached the jump. Rosie refused the uphill fence, she seemed to think it was an impossible feat to jump at the same time as climbing a hill. David shouted to Rupert, telling him to by-pass the jump and go on. They took the middle fence quite happily, but at the sight of the downhill one, Rosie's eyes bulged with horror and she stopped again. Rupert forced her on and she crept over, one leg at a time, knocking down the pole.

Oliver, complaining loudly, ran up the hill to restore the jump just in time for Lizzie, who took it cautiously and got a roar from David for looking down. Lesley had produced enough impulsion for the uphill and kept going well along the top, but when she saw the jump down she was overcome by nerves and took it from a walk. Netti went round very well. She and Tristram seemed to be full of confidence, but the other small ponies all lacked impulsion, heaving themselves over the uphill jump with difficulty and creeping downhill too carefully.

"You must get them going with more energy and impulsion," David told their riders. "Ponies don't enjoy things that are an effort to them and, by going slowly, you're making the uphill jump an effort. We want a bit more dash from you. Let's put every slow pony behind a fast one and see if we can't inspire them a bit."

When the riders tried to sort themselves out they found that there were only four fast ponies, so Lesley and Paul attached themselves to James, Lizzie and Lynne to Alice, Tina and Sarah to Netti. Rupert followed Hanif and everyone refused to follow Rupert in case he knocked down the jump again. But Rosie *was* inspired by Jupiter's example and she followed him boldly over all three jumps.

"Well done all of you," said David when the last of the smiling riders and blowing ponies had returned. "You've obviously got the hang of it now."

"Even dozey Rosie," said Oliver, patting her. "Silly old pop eyes."

"Now you can jump both slip rails. But be sensible, steady down in between them and keep off each other's tails. Wait for me in the lane."

Delighted at the thought of more jumps, they set off in a long string, the slower ponies still following their leaders. This time most people were jumping the middle of the rails

91

between the fields. Only Rupert and Tina took the lowest point, while Hanif, Alice and Paul followed James over the high end. But into the lane they were more cautious and jumped the middle.

"Mr Roberts wants all the help you can give him with course-building this afternoon," said David, when he caught up with them. "And tomorrow's the pony club rally, but I thought we'd carry on out here on the cross-country. Janet Green is going to take the younger ones in the paddock and Julia's going to give me a hand getting you over the water. All right? Can I rely on you to help Mr Roberts?"

"Yes," they answered. "We've brought our lunches."

"We'll take the ponies home and then come back here," said Lizzie.

"What time?" asked Netti.

"About an hour," said Paul, "Or an hour and a bit."

Shouting 'thank you' to David, the Wheelers and Tina clattered off down the lane. Oliver grabbed his bicycle, and shouting, "See you later!" followed.

The others ate lunch peacefully, exhausted by the morning's efforts. They were beginning to revive when Mr Roberts appeared in the yard carrying a bag of tools, and followed by Lynne and Paul laden with garden forks and spades.

"Black plastic sheet," said Mr Roberts, consulting his list. "Put that lot in the Land Rover, Paul, and fetch the sheet out of the barn. It's the one under the chaff-cutter. The rest of you come and help me with the stuff from the tractor shed. We're going to need at least a dozen fencing stakes."

They loaded the stakes, an enormous mallet, an iron bar with a sharp point for making holes, several buckets and a reel of binder twine into the Land Rover and then drove into Long Meadow to collect more poles. Then, with Sarah, Lynne and Lesley sitting in the front and everyone else crouched perilously on top of the poles, they bumped slowly along the track to Coppice Hill.

Through the slip rails they turned left and stopped beside a water trough which stood close to the hedge.

"Three poles, the plastic sheet and the buckets come off here," said Mr Roberts. "Just leave them in a pile beside the trough. We'll come back and sort it out later."

He stopped again halfway up the hill, at a little group of trees. One large, ancient elm had fallen at some time and its trunk lay sprawled across the hillside. They all got out to inspect it.

"Who can saw?" asked Mr Roberts, producing two saws from his tool bag. "David wants the middle trimmed up a bit. These branches taken off close to the trunk and no pointed or jagged bits left that could harm the ponies. He wants the boughs on the ends left alone, says they make it 'more inviting'."

"It doesn't look very inviting to me," complained Hanif.

"No, it's so solid, *and* uphill," Lesley agreed.

"Well, we can't knock it down, that's one thing," said Paul.

"I'll saw if someone will show me how," offered Alice.

"Don't you know?" they asked, shocked.

"No, it's not the sort of thing you learn in a modern flat in big cities abroad."

"Well, I'll need some diggers at the next fence—that's the ditch," said Mr Roberts. "David went round on his own yesterday evening and made us a plan."

"I'll saw," offered Hanif. "I do woodwork at school, so I can show Alice."

"Well, don't cut yourselves."

"There's nothing to it," said Hanif as the Land Rover went on up the hill, "you just saw. I have to do woodwork because my stepfather disapproves of people who are only good at normal lessons. He says I'll turn into a swot."

"Well I suppose it *is* useful to be able to make things." Alice chose a thin straggly bough and started work. "I don't know how to do anything useful. Aunt Margaret says she'll teach me to cook."

They sawed. The angles were awkward, the branches

scratched them and when the sun came out the day was suddenly hot. They stopped for a rest and took off their anoraks. Then they sawed again until they heard voices and the four Wheelers and Tina appeared, puffing up the hill.

"The bikes are all bust up and we had to walk the whole way," complained Oliver, collapsing on the short, cowslip-studded turf.

"What are you doing?" asked Netti.

"Sawing," answered Alice.

"We can see that."

"We're making this tree trunk jumpable. It's part of David's course," Hanif told them.

"It's wide."

"And jolly solid."

"Are we going to jump it uphill?"

"I hope so," answered Hanif. "Are any of you good at sawing? My arms are aching."

Lizzie and Netti took over.

"You need a chain saw," said Rupert, collapsing on the grass beside Oliver, "then it would be done in a second."

"And a bulldozer to dig a ditch, I suppose," suggested Hanif.

"That's not a ditch they're digging," said Rupert with conviction. "It's a communal grave for pony club members who expire from too much exercise."

"I think I'll go and see if they need help," decided Tina. "It's no use having seven people for two saws."

Oliver followed her. Alice was looking at the view, over Garland Farm and Four Cross to Woodbury and the river. And, beyond the river, to the beechwoods, coloured purple by the millions of unopened buds. "We're on top of the world," she said to Hanif.

"Not bad is it," he answered, turning to look as he threaded the sawn-off branches among the ones they had been told to leave at either end. "I wish I could fix Jupe up with a hang glider and we could both drift gently home."

"Here, you two take over again," demanded Netti. "My arms are completely worn out. Are yours, Lizzie?"

When the sawing was done they all walked on slowly to the ditch. Paul and Sarah, Tina and James were all digging or shovelling energetically.

"Not very impressive," said Rupert, looking at it critically. "I expected it to be several feet deep, but you've only managed a few inches."

"See if you can do any better," answered James, handing him a fork.

"It's all stones and very hard work," Sarah told him.

"And anyway, it's meant to be shallow, only six inches deep, because it's *introducing* the ponies to ditches," Paul added defensively. "David said he didn't want them all falling in and frightening themselves into fits."

"Quite right," said Hanif, taking Sarah's spade. "We don't want the riders falling in either—but why are we piling the earth on the far side like this?"

"Some idea of Dad's," answered Paul. "And he's coming back to rivet the ditch when he's finished knocking posts in over there."

Assisted by Oliver and Lesley, Mr Roberts had taken down a section of the wire fence between the two fields and was knocking in four posts to make a frame. "We're going to fill this up with brushwood and greenery," he explained. "So while I'm nailing these lengths of timber across, some of you can go collecting branches in the wood. No yew or we'll be losing the cattle. It only takes the smallest bit of yew to kill an animal, and dead yew's even more lethal than when it's green. But you'll find plenty of box and laurel."

The Wheelers, Lynne and Tina all decided that they wanted to branch collect, and set off armed with the saws and some secateurs. Alice joined the digging party. James and Paul were taking the ditch very seriously and insisting on straight edges, and Mr Roberts was pleased when he arrived with Lesley, both of them carrying tools.

"Fine," he said. "Just the job. I'm going to put this pole along the take-off side and fix it there with a couple of short posts knocked into the ditch. Otherwise, if the ponies start refusing and messing about, the edge will crumble away and you won't have a take-off. Now, we want something for the far side so they know it's a jump. By rights it should be a brush fence, but I spotted a fallen tree in the little copse over there, just a small one, and it's been lying there a good while so it won't be heavy. Will you go and see if you can fetch it over, while Lesley and I get on with this?"

James didn't think much of the log. "Far too small," he complained. "Ferdie will trip over it."

"It would do under a pole," suggested Alice.

"Help heave," said James. "It weighs a ton."

Mr Roberts was delighted with the log, and when it was embedded in the bank of earth they had dug out, it looked quite impressive.

"It's terrifying," said Hanif, standing back to inspect the fence. "You can't tell that it's not a real ditch; I'm sure they'll all refuse."

"It does look awfully wide," agreed Alice, joining him. "I think they'll all fall in."

"Right, back to the little copse," said Mr Roberts, producing his plan.

As they climbed through the wire fence, the greenery collecting party appeared on the edge of the wood, dragging branches and shrieking cheerfully.

"Three poles and baling string," said Mr Roberts, observing that his helpers had all begun to wish themselves in the wood. "David's marked the trees we're to tie the poles to with an X in chalk."

They found the marked trees. The first two pairs made an angle jump, the third pair were on the very edge of the coppice, and as the hill fell away steeply at that point, you seemed to be jumping right out into space.

"Ugh, it's horrible," said Alice.

"Do you think David would notice if we moved it back a bit?" asked Hanif.

"Yes, of course he would. Don't be so *wet*. Your pony's a first class jumper, but you never stop moaning," James told him irritably.

"It's called Horizon Fence on the plan," said Paul. "How high, Dad?"

"About two feet six. Tie the baling string round the tree at about three foot and then make a loop for the pole," instructed Mr Roberts.

"I don't suppose we'll ever get this far," Alice comforted Hanif when James wasn't listening. "I can't see many of us getting over the ditch."

They walked back to the Land Rover. The wood party were filling the frame with branches and giving cries of horror at the height of the jump.

"That's great," James told them. "Don't squash it down too much, we want one decent-sized fence."

"Well, none of *us* are going to get over that," said Rupert, squashing hard.

"Squash it down to start with," suggested Sarah. "We can always make it higher later."

"At least it's on the flat," observed Hanif.

"Now, down to the gate in the corner there," said Mr Roberts, pointing to the far end of the field where a five-barred gate led to the sunken lane. "Anyone want to ride down?"

James, Rupert and Lesley made for the Land Rover. Everyone else began to run down the hill, pretending to be nervous riders on badly behaved, runaway ponies. Only Alice proceeded at a collected pace, roaring, "Legs!" and "Look up!" in a David-like manner. Lynne jumped the pole on the drums and then fell, lying in a giggling heap, until Hanif announced that it was tetanus and he was about to inject her, when she made an instant recovery.

The Land Rover party were behaving much more soberly. Mr Roberts and James were tying a pole across the gateway while Rupert, who had insisted on a turn with the mallet, was narrowly missing Lesley with every blow he took at a reluctant post.

"I suppose it's a bounce fence," he said gloomily, "but with the second pole on the edge of a drop into the lane, Rosie's bound to fall on her nose."

"Look what you're doing!" Lesley shrieked at him angrily. "You only just missed my hand that time. Oh, Mr Roberts, do come and knock this one in. Rupert's quite hopeless."

Mr Roberts knocked in the two posts with a few effortless strokes. "Right, you can tie the second pole on. Two feet high, David says."

"There's not enough room to land on the bank," objected Rupert.

"It is a bit tricky," James admitted. "Not much room for manoeuvre if you've got a big one like Ferdie; the little ponies will be all right."

"We seem to have lost the rest of our gang," said Mr Roberts as the four of them climbed back into the Land Rover.

"They're over by the water trough," Lesley told him. "I can hear my sister's voice. I expect they're tired of working and are just fooling around."

But when they drove into the schooling field they found great activity going on; everyone seemed to be dragging logs and boughs and tree trunks from the hedges and woods.

"We're building a stick heap," shouted Oliver to Rupert.

"A logpile," Netti corrected him.

"We thought we'd show some initiative and give David a surprise," explained Hanif. "Please will you add it to the plan, Mr Roberts? We're building it between the water and the tree trunk."

"I'll wait till I've seen the final result," answered Mr Roberts unenthusiastically. "We could do with a couple more helpers down here. Paul, come and give me a hand with this sheet," he called. "And we need another digger."

Lizzie came running and offered to be the fourth digger.

"It's easier here than on top of the hill," James told her. "Far less stones."

"It's been churned to mud by the cattle coming to drink," said Lesley. "If you'll loosen, Lizzie, I'll shovel."

They scraped and shovelled energetically. Ten feet by

five, Mr Roberts had ordered, and with the earth piled at either end, but as there was a natural dip in the field, they didn't have to dig very deep. Mr Roberts and Paul shook out the plastic sheet, folded it to a suitable size, and they all fitted into the hollow. They wound the spare ends round two heavy poles to hold it on the landing and take-off sides and weighed it down with earth at either end. Then they grabbed buckets and began to fling water in it from the trough, wondering if it would hold. It seemed to take an incredible number of bucketsful to even cover the sheet. Mr Roberts left them to it and went to inspect the log jump. Alice and Netti were trying to build the untidy heap into an orderly-looking jump with the largest logs at the bottom.

"Not bad, is it?" asked Alice.

"Not *bad*? It's brilliant," Nettie told her.

"I'll knock in a couple of posts and put a pole across to make it solid," said Mr Roberts, "otherwise the ponies'll start dragging their legs through it, and you'll spend half the morning building it up."

They helped Mr Roberts with the posts and pole, but everyone else had lost interest in the log pile and drifted down to the water.

"It's horrible. Chess simply won't go near it, I know he won't," wailed Sarah.

"Well, at least you won't shoot into it head first," said Hanif. "I'm convinced that will be my fate."

"And mine," agreed Rupert. "I can just see Rosie coming to one of her shuddering halts."

"I hope the sheet's watertight," said Paul. "It's going to be a bit of a disaster if it all drains away in the night."

"I think it would be quite a good idea to *start* with it empty," said Lizzie. "Less wet for falling into and we could fill it up later."

CHAPTER SIX

Fainthearts and Lionhearts

"I decided that I'd rather help David than ride in the rally," Oliver explained to the other pony club members when they met at the water on Wednesday morning.

"It's lost about three inches in the night," said James, intent on the jump. "If you wouldn't mind holding Ferdie for a couple of minutes, Alice, I'll fill it up."

"I can't stand that Janet Green," Oliver went on. "She must be the most boring instructor that ever existed. You spend at *least* half the rally touching your toes. *And* she only gives about two for turnout."

"That's generous," Netti told him, "considering that Hobbit's always caked in mud and you never clean your tack or your boots."

"Julia always gives me at *least* five," replied Oliver haughtily. "Anyway, it means that Tina can have Hobbit and I'll find out whether he can jump ditches and water."

"We're all going to find that out. The moment of truth is here," said Hanif gloomily. "I've brought some dry clothes."

As the Land Rover bumped into the field, they saw that Mrs Rooke, looking severe and wearing a brown macintosh and matching hat, despite the sunshine, was sitting beside David. Several people remembered that Sarah and Lesley were there just in time to choke back their groans.

"Good morning, all," said David, coming to a halt beside the water. "That looks very wet. I expect we shall have a mighty splash or two this afternoon."

"Chess won't go near it. I've tried to lead him up, but he won't move a step. I'm never going to get over." Sarah sounded indignant.

"Perhaps Sarah could have Lesley's pony for the water,"

100

suggested Mrs Rooke. "It's rather hard on her to have a pony with a real phobia about black plastic, and Lesley doesn't really care about jumping."

"Well, let's deal with the problems as we come to them," said David. "We'll begin by schooling."

The schooling went well that morning. The ponies were all becoming more supple and energetic and the riders, feeling the improvement, felt they were getting somewhere and cheerfully tried harder still. Rosie was allowed to join in the leg-yielding for the first time and seemed to understand it immediately. Rupert said that she had been watching the other ponies, but David insisted that it was Rupert who had been watching and was therefore able to explain clearly what he wanted.

They cantered a lot. David told them to make the school bigger by going wide, outside the markers, and then to increase their speed along the long sides and slow up on the short ones. He was soon shouting, "Go on, gallop!" as they hurtled along the long sides and, "Steady!" at some people who were failing to slow up for the short ones. The ponies enjoyed it tremendously; the fast ones enjoyed showing off their speed and the slow ones were enlivened by the company. When the time came to halt they all pulled up with pricked ears and shining eyes.

"Very good." said David. "Do you all begin to see that it's a lively but controllable pony we're trying to produce by our schooling? We don't want a meek, dreary animal creeping round, and we don't want a sullen animal that's been mastered by force. Obedience must be something that the pony agrees to willingly and cheerfully; there must be nothing slavish about it."

He turned back towards the Land Rover. "Right then, off you go along the valley. The people who want to jump the slip rails at full height go first. The Land Rover party will lower them for the rest of you."

James set off steadily, followed by Hanif, Alice, Netti and Paul. The Rookes and Lizzie dithered.

"Wait till we've put it down and then jump at the high

end," David told them as he watched the first five ponies fly over.

Oliver managed to make the lowered rails a little higher by adding a broken rail as a cross pole and all the ponies jumped confidently.

"Twice round the easy way at the canter," said David when everyone had arrived in the second field, "and either half-halt or trot before the downhill jump. Keep your distances and if anything goes wrong ahead of you, stop."

They set off, a long string of riders all enjoying themselves; it had become so easy and the ponies had become partners instead of opponents.

David had struggled up on to the Land Rover bonnet and was sitting beside Oliver, loudhailer in hand. Mrs Rooke stood a little apart, watching in amazement.

"I can't get over it," she said as pony after pony popped over the downhill jump and halted beside the flag. "What have you done to them, David? I know Sarah, James and Netti were quite good little riders, but the *rest* of them! I can't imagine how you've done it, I really can't."

"It shows there was nothing wrong with them. They were quite willing to work at it when they had someone to tell them what to do." David picked up the loudhailer to roar "Legs!" at Lynne. "I must say I'm quite pleased with them."

"I should think so," said Mrs Rooke. "They all look as though they'd been riding cross-country for years and even that dreadful pony the Wheelers bought for Rupert is going in the right direction for a change."

"Round the harder way, once," David told James as the last pony halted at the flag. "And Lizzie, do remember to look up."

"I never thought you'd teach that mutton-fisted little Harry Franklin to ride; when I saw him that first morning at the rally my heart failed, but look at him now!" said Mrs Rooke, her magnified eyes full of admiration.

"Well done," David told the pony club members as Tina, who had been the last one to go, joined the group. "You've

102

all got good cross-country seats and you all know how to jump downhill. And I'm pleased with the ponies too; the idle ones are going with a lot more impulsion, the wild ones have calmed down, and they're all on the bit most of the time. They also seem quite a lot fitter than when we started."

The pony club members looked at each other. It was something to have satisfied David, they thought, patting their ponies self-consciously.

"Now you can all jump the slip rail and wait for me by the tree trunk. Full height for everyone this time, so will those who are doubtful take a good lead."

Inspired by leads and encouraged by the fact that they were heading homewards, the ponies jumped willingly. Only Rosie, going last, almost refused and then made an enormous leap.

"There's nothing to tree trunks," said David, catching up with his ride. "They're solid, straightforward and natural, ponies understand them. This one is slightly uphill, so you make sure that you have plenty of impulsion."

Only Rupert was worried by the tree trunk, everyone else was longing to get at it. They rode fast and with determination and the ponies sailed over. Rosie made one of her huge leaps.

"Over the logpile and then over the tree trunk again," shouted David.

The ponies were less certain about the logpile. Even Ferdinand and Saffron took large careful leaps over it. Banjo made one of his stag jumps, high into the air, Star-dust refused, so did Berry, Chess and Rajah. Only Jupiter and Tristram seemed completely unconcerned.

"Form up the ride again," said David. "Will the ponies that have got over give leads. Now come on, it's not a big jump and I think it's the riders who are being faint-hearted."

When they got going again, the ponies' courage rose and they followed their leaders over. Then all the refusers were sent round on their own.

"Now for the ditch," said David, struggling back into the Land Rover. By the time he had driven up the hill the riders were gathered round the ditch, all looking anxious and slightly green.

"Do any of the ponies jump ditches?" he asked. "James?"

"Ferdies done them in riding club competitions with my mother, but he generally had a stop or even two; they're definitely not his strong point."

"Anyone else?" asked David.

"Only those little ones at the side of the road," said Netti "but Tristram jumps most things."

"I have a feeling a Crankshaw pony living at Waterford farm won't be too bothered about ditches or water, so we'll send Alice first, then James and Harry and Netti, Paul and Lizzie. After that we'll see," David decided. "Now it's wide but not high, and what height there is is on the far side, so obviously you take off as near to the ditch as you can, which means you come fairly fast and with a light contact—a giving hand. *Don't* jump it as though it were a stile or a gate, *don't* stand back, jump it as you would a triple."

Alice wasn't very happy about her position as leader, but she gritted her teeth and tried to convince Saffron that she knew all about jumping ditches and to her surprise it worked. He jumped it easily. Behind her Ferdinand made a last minute run out, but Jupiter thundered on and jumped, without hesitating. Tristram followed him, Banjo stopped, looked, and then jumped, unseating Paul, who clung round his neck, but managed to get back into the saddle on the far side. Rajah refused, peering down into the ditch with a disapproving expression.

"Clear the course," ordered David. "We'll now have the people who haven't tried, but with leads. James, you don't need a lead, just be ready for him this time and keep him straight."

Lesley followed Alice, but at rather a half-hearted pace, and then slithered nervously on the edge of the ditch.

"Take her away," shouted David as Jupiter thundered

up with Rosie on his tail. A great cheer went up as she followed him over.

"I don't think she saw the ditch," said Rupert, patting her profusely. "I think she thought it was just another log with some earth lying about."

The fact that Rosie was over encouraged several people who had been certain that they would never make it, and though Chess, Berry and Hobbit refused, they all three had a look and then went over at their second attempts. Rupert offered Lizzie a lead in a very lordly manner and, much to his amazement, Rosie again jumped the ditch easily. Rajah followed.

Only Stardust was left, she was still cantering up slowly with her ears back and obviously had no intention of jumping.

"Go on, Lesley. Wake her up, get her over," called Mrs Rooke in exasperated tones. "Give her a good whack, don't just sit there, kick."

"You'd better put Sarah up," she told David: "she's the one with the drive. We'll be here all night if we wait for Lesley to get the pony over."

"This little mare is a bit faint-hearted, she lacks self-confidence," said David, limping forward to give Stardust a consoling pat. "I don't think kicking and whacking are the answer. Ponies are so very different; old Jupiter is a real lionheart, prepared to take on anything, but Stardust's at the opposite end of the scale; she's a bit of a softie and you'll get most out of her by building up her confidence and encouraging her."

Hanif was patting Jupiter's liver chestnut neck. "Jupe the Lionheart," he announced, pleased with the compliment.

"I think Saffron's quite lionhearted too," said Alice.

"Yes," David agreed, "but he's the sort of pony which needs a partner, he has to like and trust his rider. Jupiter would cart anyone over anything; he relies on himself."

"That is perfectly true," said Hanif, remembering the Brunstock show.

"What about Ra?" asked Lizzie.

"He's cautious by nature. If he was a person he would insure everything. He disapproves of taking risks."

"And Chess?"

"Like so many small ponies which have belonged to little children, he doesn't have much respect for his rider. He thinks *he* knows best and he likes to take a look at the jumps before he attempts them; you've got to convince him you're grown-up.

"Now I want you to form up the ride again. All go down and start over the logpile, then the tree trunk and then the ditch. Alice, I want you and Lesley at the back."

Everyone but Lesley was delighted to be jumping a piece of the course. They jogged down the hill arguing about leads. Lesley patted Startdust. The furious anger she'd felt at her mother's interference had cooled when David had told her she was wrong. And of course he was right, it was no use kicking and hitting a pony or person who lacked confidence. She patted Stardust again. "You're just as good as the rest of them. Don't worry, just copy Saffron."

James and Ferdinand came racing up the hill looking very pleased with themselves as they sailed over the ditch. David shouted, "Go on, over the brush, keep going."

He roared the same message at the other riders as they jumped the ditch and one by one they went on, swooping over the brush with ease.

The later riders could see what was happening. "If Stardust refuses, let's go on and jump the brush," Alice suggested to Lesley as they set off. But this time Stardust's blood was up; she was excited as she chased Saffron and the flying ponies ahead, and followed them over the ditch and then the brush without thought of refusing.

The riders all patted their ponies delightedly.

"I never thought Rosie would jump as high as that," Rupert told everyone who would listen.

"It's at least three feet to the top leaf," said Sarah, who had dismounted and was measuring the fence against herself.

"Angles," said David, leaving the Land Rover on the

106

edge of the trees and limping towards the two jumps. "The most important thing is to *look* where you want to go. Your head is very heavy and, as you know, the rider's weight is an aid, so by turning your head and shoulders in the direction you want to go you give the pony a clear signal. If you look straight ahead or down at the ground when you want to turn, you're giving the pony a totally incorrect signal; it's your fault if he doesn't get over the second fence. Point him at the first fence, but *look at* and *think about* the second one. O.K.? Start slowly, but with impulsion. If you go too fast the pony won't have time to adjust his stride and you may have a refusal. As all our ponies are novices we're not going to cut corners or go the shortest way; that comes later. So pop over the first, ride at the second, circle left and come back here."

With all the riders staring rigidly in the correct direction, the ponies found the little jumps perfectly simple and only Berry ran out of the second one.

"Now for the horizon," said David when Lynne was over at her second attempt. "Ours is very small and easy, but you can see that if you came galloping at some great hairy brush fence set on the hill like that, your pony might easily think, 'Good grief there's nowhere to land,' and you'd have a last-minute refusal. The secret of jumping all tricky fences is to approach slowly but with impulsion. And that's why they have them in competition courses; they want to test the pony's training. Unschooled horses can only maintain impulsion by going fast. So pop over, look right, circle the coppice and come back here. If you look straight down the hill you'll probably find yourself going there."

James and Alice jumped it easily. Hanif, looking right with desperate concentration, found it worked; Jupiter made no attempt to run away down the hill. Rosie and Stardust refused, but both jumped at their second try. The little ponies popped over eagerly, wondering what all the fuss was about. Then David sent them all back with instructions to jump the brush, angle and horizon fences one after the other. Everyone was pleased, their worries and fears

107

had all vanished—it was fun and the ponies, enjoying it too, didn't need much riding.

"Down to the gate into the lane," said David, making his way back to the Land Rover.

They rode down on loose reins, chattering. Oliver walked proudly beside Hobbit.

"Isn't he going *well*?" he asked Tina. "I never thought he'd do the big ones like the ditch and the brush."

"He's great," agreed Tina, "so brave; he's another lionheart. I'm having a lovely time, Ollie, thanks to you. I've learned more about riding in these three days than in my whole life."

"David's good, isn't he? I can't wait to get into his ride."

"Now," said David, gathering them round the gateway, "this is a test of the pony's cleverness and agility and, of course, impulsion. Think about the second fence and look the way you want to turn in the lane, and go slowly so that the pony has a chance to see what he's got to do. O.K., James. This time we'll turn left on landing. Don't follow too closely as some people are bound to get stuck."

Ferninand, looking very serious, jumped it perfectly. Rajah and Banjo followed him carefully. Jupiter flung himself over the first one, landed too near the second and had to turn round before he could jump down into the lane.

"That'll teach him to look before he leaps," shouted David. "Combinations are very good for over-confident ponies."

Saffron went over neatly, but Rosie over-jumped the first one, refused the second, then changed her mind and decided she could jump it from a standstill, but hit the pole so hard with her hindlegs that she broke the baling string.

"Oh, dozy Rosie, you make more work than all the others put together," complained Oliver, hurrying to repair the damage.

Then Tristram led the small ponies over and they all found it quite easy because they could fit in so many strides. Last of all Stardust jumped in and then spent several minutes teetering on the bank before she summoned the courage to jump down into the lane, which she did from a standstill.

"Now you can come back," David shouted through the loudhailer. "You'll need some impulsion to get up the bank. Go a bit further up the lane so that you've room to get going. Then keep as near to the left hand hedge as you can so you give yourself the maximum turning space, and don't take your pony by surprise."

Ferdinand *was* rather surprised, but he climbed over somehow, and the other ponies following knew they had to jump. Rajah heaved himself over with a great grunt, Banjo did one of his stage-like springs, vertically into the air. Berry and Chess gave their riders uncomfortable, slow motion jumps and Rosie climbed over the pole one leg at a time. Saffron jumped it well; Stardust followed without refusing and Hobbit, coming last, flew over in the neatest possible manner.

"We'll do it into the lane again," said David, "but this time I want you to turn the opposite way to the pony in front of you. James, you'll go to the right, so if you're next, Lizzie, you'll turn left, Paul right and so on, all down the line. Does everyone understand? I want to see that you're in charge, not the ponies."

Only Rosie went the wrong way; she made such an awkward jump that Rupert was in no position to steer. Sarah and Lynne were giving shrieks of dismay as they jumped, but managed to turn their separate ways. Then they all leapt back into the field in fine style, finding that the bank was perfectly easy if you had enough impulsion.

"A volunteer to give Rosie one more lead," said David, and chose Lizzie from all the shouted offers.

"Now lunch," he said when the Wheelers returned. "You can jump both slip rails on the way in, but don't go mad. James, will you hold everyone up in the lane until the last one's over."

"What a morning!" said Hanif, settling contentedly to his lunch, when all the ponies had been watered, fed and tied up in the barn, out of kicking distance of each other.

"I'm glad it's only us and all that dreary D lot have gone home," remarked Oliver, munching pork pie.

"You're a dreary D yourself," Paul told him. He and Lynne had persuaded their mother to let them eat their lunch in the barn with the other pony club members.

"I may be a D, but I'm not dreary," Oliver told him fiercely.

"Mummy thinks we've improved out of all recognition," announced Sarah, who had been collecting her lunch from Mrs Rooke's car. "*She* thinks we're quite good enough to go in for the Area Cup and she's going to persuade David to relent and let us enter. She's gone home now, but she's going to ring him tonight when he's had a rest."

"It'll be too late," said Lizzie. "The entries will have closed!"

"That's what I said, but being an efficient secretary she entered a team at the very beginning of the holidays, before David decided we would disgrace him."

"Oh *no*," groaned Hanif, his contentment vanishing. "We don't want to spoil everything with teams and prizes and having to win."

"There's no need to get worked up," Rupert told him. "O.K., she's entered a team, but that's only five people; you don't have to be in it."

"He's one of the best at cross-country," James pointed out.

"But not much good at dressage," added Sarah quickly.

"He'd be good for turn-out though," observed Lynne. "Jupiter always looks lovely and his tack is practically new."

"Thank you," said Hanif, "but I don't want to be in it. I renounce any claim I may have."

"Mummy wants Jennifer to be in it," Sarah told them.

"Why? She isn't on the course," protested Paul. "She thought she was too good."

"Well, that's the point isn't it?" said James. "She's the best rider in the Woodbury and she knows it."

"My mother will want James, Jennifer, the Great Sarah,

Netti and a Roberts," Lesley told Alice. "She settled it months ago; I expect she'll get her own way."

Lynne had produced a quiz book. "We'd better practise," she said, "just in case."

"It's not fair to ask questions out of that book. Both you and Sarah know all the answers by heart," Paul objected.

"Oh come on, it's not a competition, it's just for fun," Sarah told him. "Will you quiz us, James?"

"It's not my idea of fun," said Rupert, retreating to a distant straw bale.

James swallowed down a sandwich and opened the book obediently.

"Name two plants which are poisonous to horses," he demanded.

"Yew."

"Deadly Nightshade."

"Privet."

"Rhododendrons."

"Ivy," they shouted all at once.

"Spaghetti," said Rupert. Sarah gave him a withering look. "Let's go over there in the corner," she suggested to her team mates. "And James, you must ask us each a question in turn and give us marks for a correct or semi-correct answer."

"What do the following initials stand for?" asked James. "B.H.S."

"Beastly. Horrible. Stinking!" shouted Oliver.

"Oh, shut up. Can't you understand that we want to have a good team for a change?" snapped Sarah. "We want to beat the Cranford Vale even if you don't."

"Leave them alone, Ollie. It's not fair to spoil their practice!" Lizzie told him.

"Jokes are only funny once," Rupert added. "It's boring to go on and on."

"I *wasn't* going on and on," objected Oliver.

The team soon grew tired of their question master. James was very slow and deliberate and insisted looking up all the answers in the back of the book though Lynne and

111

Sarah knew they had given the correct ones. They began to discuss what they should call themselves. Sarah and Lynne wanted to be The Woodbury Wonders, Netti said it sounded a bit boastful and she thought they ought to wait until they had done something wonderful before they gave themselves a name like that.

"We could have T shirts with it printed on the front," suggested Lynne.

"Well, if Jennifer's going to be in the team we'd better wait and ask her what she thinks," said James, "but I think we should just be the Woodbury, or Woodbury P.C."

"I knew all this talk of teams would spoil the atmosphere," Hanif complained to Alice as they bridled their ponies. "They are going to divide us into two lots."

"It's only Sarah," Alice told him. "I'm sure Netti and James and the Robertses aren't like that."

"Teams can ruin people's natures," said Hanif gloomily.

Some of the pony club members were still tacking up when David drove the Land Rover into the yard.

"Come on, get moving," he told them. "Julia will be waiting at Coppice Hill and we've got to get you all over that water before dark."

"I know I'm *never* going to get over it," wailed Sarah. "Not even if we stay there all night."

"Where are my dry clothes?" demanded Hanif, looking round.

"You left them under the hedge by the water jump," Alice reminded him.

They were all rather silent as they rode down the farm track. Quite a few people had hollow-feeling stomachs and weak legs at the thought of the water, and these feelings grew worse when they found Julia waiting for them, armed with a lunge rein and lungeing whip.

"We'll warm up by jumping the slip rail into the second field and then doing the hill the easy way," said David. "Do it well, because I want to show Julia how you've come on. Let the slow ponies chase a fast one and don't forget to halt at the final flag. Off you go, James."

They felt much more on their own, starting from the first field and with no David and main group of ponies waiting below in the valley, but they all enjoyed the feeling of being alone with their ponies and the long string of ponies and riders looked very impressive as it snaked up and down the hill in a controlled manner.

"I'm stunned," said Julia when they had all come back. "Truthfully. I never thought you could improve that much in three days, even with David cursing you. They'll all go straight over the water, won't they?" she asked. "You won't need me and my gear."

"Yes we will. I'm told we have one confirmed hater of black plastic among the ponies and several of the riders have made up their minds to refuse."

"The water's gone down two inches," reported James. "Shall I fill it up?"

"*No!*" the other pony club members shrieked at him.

"No," agreed David. "There's plenty there for our purpose, but I would like a pole over the centre. The long one, resting on a couple of drums on their sides. James, give Julia a hand."

"That makes it worse," complained Netti.

"*Much* worse," agreed Lynne.

"It makes it easier for the ponies," David told them. "They realise it's a jump and don't fall in and it protects my plastic sheet from the ones that want to wade through. Now, has anyone a pony that's jumped water?"

"Well Ferdie *has*, but he doesn't like it much," answered James. "He generally has a stop or two with my mother at the riding club."

"Let's try Alice in the lead then," said David. "Come at a brisk pace, Alice, but the important thing is to increase your speed during the last few strides. Some riders start too fast and run out of steam as they get there, that's fatal. Harry, you're second, James third. Then anyone else who feels they *might* make it. We deal with the difficult ones later."

Alice cantered a circle and approached briskly. Saffron

saw the jump, pricked his ears, lengthened his stride and flew over effortlessly. Everyone cheered, he made it look so easy. Hanif had turned and was riding in pursuit. Jupiter made an enormous leap, far higher and wider than was necessary, but it was a smooth jump and Hanif sat tight. James followed grim-faced. He rode in a very determined manner but, at the very last moment, Ferdinand's heart failed, he braked violently, skidded to a halt on the very brink, head down, almost tipping in. James went on, landing with a loud splash on the far side, the bottom half of him in the water.

There were cries of horror which turned to laughter as James crawled out and then stood looking ruefully at his dripping jodhs.

"Oh Ferdie, you brute," he said and then began to laugh too.

"You can have my spare jodhs," offered Hanif. "They are stretch ones."

"I'm all right, I'll soon dry out."

"You won't, you know." Julia, who'd caught Ferdinand, took a closer look. "You're sopping and you won't do your mother's beautiful saddle any good."

"O.K.," James agreed, "I'd better see if I can get into them."

The two boys went off together, Hanif to retrieve his clothes from their hiding place in the hedge, James to find a bush he could change behind.

David shouted, "Next!" at the riders, none of whom felt the least desire to be next in the water but Lizzie, always obliging, stirred Rajah into a canter. He approached as slowly as possible, a highly disapproving expression on his long chestnut face, and with obviously no intention of jumping.

Lizzie let him inspect the water, he sniffed it suspiciously and then gave a loud snort.

"Take him away," said David. "He knows all about it, you showed it to him this morning; he's just putting on an act. Anyone else want a go?"

Lesley rode up flapping her legs, but not throwing her heart over. Paul came fast but let Banjo run out at the last moment.

"I think Tristram would do it, but could we have a lead?" asked Netti. "All this falling off and refusing has unnerved us."

David called for Alice. "Put them over the log pile and then circle round and over the water," he instructed.

"Hurry up, Harry! We need you," called Julia.

Harry came trotting back. "Everything's a bit tight," he said, giggling, "but he's got into the jodhs and the socks."

"I'll need a leg-up," complained James, following at a stiff-legged walk. "I can't bend my knees."

Alice and Netti leapt the log pile, swept round and sailed over the water with no problems at all.

"It looks so easy when they do it," wailed Lynne.

"It *is* easy," David told her. "The difficulties are all in the minds of the riders and ponies. All right, Harry and James. And be ready for him this time, James."

"I will," James shouted back, as, brandishing his whip, they rode at the log pile. And, though Ferdinand made a large and apprehensive-looking jump and James, determined not to go over his head again, got left behind, they reached the far bank safely.

"Do it once more," shouted David. "Paul, you follow them."

This time James and Ferdinand jumped well, but Banjo made another of his last-minute run-outs.

"Very bad," shouted David. "Anyone can be taken by surprise, but to let a pony run out twice to the same side is bad riding. You must tell him with reins and legs before you start that he's not going to do it; turn him into the hedge, have a dead refusal. You see if they come up to a fence with a run-out in mind they don't make any plans for jumping, they don't think about the take-off, so you don't have a hope of getting over. Come once more on your own, Paul, and *make* him do a dead refusal."

While Paul was trying to convince Banjo that he wasn't

going to run out again, David asked Julia and Oliver to make a wing. They placed a large oil drum on the non-hedge side of the water and rested one end of a pole on it and the other on a small drum.

"Don't think that a wing will do your work for you," said David, "it won't, but it may help a bit. Right, Alice, give him another lead."

This time Banjo refused and then, before Paul could turn him away, he made an enormous leap from a standstill. Paul shot out of the saddle, clung round the pony's neck, and then fell off on the far side, just clear of the water.

The riders of the other small ponies became even more glum.

"I don't think we're ever going to do it," said Tina. "It's too wide for little ponies."

"If Banjo won't, Berry hasn't a hope," agreed Lynne.

"I always knew it was a waste of time even *trying* with Chess," complained Sarah. "Why doesn't David let us go round the whole course on our own? That would be much more fun."

"If there's a lead going, I will be the next sacrificial victim," offered Rupert suddenly.

"Good. We'll have Netti and James, just to make sure their ponies are really happy about it, then Harry and Rupert, then Alice and Paul."

Tristram was obviously perfectly happy, but Ferdinand was still jumping carefully. Then Harry and Rupert, who'd warmed up over the log pile, came in fast and Rosie didn't seem to notice the water. Chasing Jupiter, she sailed over as though it was only the pole she had to jump. Everyone cheered and clapped.

Flinging himself off, Rupert hugged her enthusiastically and then began to beg bread and pony nuts from anyone who had some left in his or her pocket. "Do you think she actually saw the water?" he asked David anxiously.

"Yes, I expect she jumped streams as foal, followed her dam over; she doesn't understand what all the fuss is about. Now where's Paul? James, you can give him another lead and then we'll start using the Irish method on the rest of them."

"Can Lesley and I have one more lead?" asked Lizzie, who was rather annoyed that her brother and sister were over.

"Yes, O.K., but neither of you looked very hopeful," said David, watching Paul. Banjo made another enormous leap, but this time Paul was ready for him and stayed on. Then Lesley and Lizzie came with their leads but, though they both looked very determined and, kicking and whacking with a windmill of arms and legs, tried to make their ponies jump from a standstill, they couldn't get over.

"What *are* you supposed to do when your pony just *won't* jump?" asked Lizzie despondently.

"I'm going to show you one method, which seems to work well over ditches and water," answered David, as Julia passed the lunge rein through one ring of Rajah's snaffle and buckled it to the other.

"Try and see it from the pony's point of view," he went on, raising his voice and talking to all the members. "There's this horrible jump and you have to decide how to get over it, where to take off and how high and how wide you ought to jump. If you get it wrong you can fall, bang your legs, drown. Bad enough without a rider, but when you've got one of them, all your troubles are doubled. They whack you and kick you when you're trying to work out the take-off, their weight tips all over the place, unbalancing you when you're dithering on the brink, trying to get up the courage for an enormous leap, and, if you finally make the enormous leap, they go and fall off. Now we're going to try without riders. Cross your stirrups, Lizzie."

"I want you to lead him up to it," Julia told Lizzie, "then I'll tow him over it from the far side. Be ready to stand clear when he jumps."

"*If* he jumps," Lizzie corrected her.

Rajah dithered and teetered for several minutes while Julia pulled gently and Lizzie and David made encouraging noises.

"Jump over yourself, Lizzie, or wade through. Show him that even humans can do it," called David.

Lizzie scrambled and hopped across, trying to keep her leaking boot out of the water, and then called Rajah from the far side. His dithering increased, but his eyes had stopped rolling with obstinacy.

"He's going," said David and everyone began to shout encouraging remarks. Suddenly Rajah made a huge leap and found himself being praised and patted and rewarded from a scoop of oats on the far side.

Lizzie led him back for a second attempt and this time he only dithered for a moment, and the third time he didn't dither at all.

"Now Lesley," said David.

Stardust made less fuss than Rajah, and Hobbit, who went next, made no fuss at all. Berry was more difficult. Always inclined to kick, she lashed out angrily at anyone who went near her and kept charging into the wing rather than face the water. Julia gave the lunge rein to Lizzie, with instructions to move back quickly if Berry show signs of coming over, and, taking the lunge whip, stood outside the wing and kept the pony straight. Furious, Berry sulked. She stood, ears back, with a mulish expression, and refused to budge. Julia began to tap her on the quarters with the lunge whip, Lynne shook the scoop of oats invitingly on the far side. Berry stood and sulked, but the annoying tapping of the whip went on and the oats became more tempting; suddenly she gave in and jumped with the greatest of ease. At her second attempt she went over with no trouble at all. Lynne was amazed and delighted.

"Now, let's have those four ponies over, mounted," said David. "The rest of you can give them leads. Make a sort of hunt of it; we want them to enjoy themselves. Then we'll deal with Master Chess."

The ten ponies were soon racing over the logpile and the water. Pony after pony flew over happily. Only Berry misbehaved, jumping the wing, but when Lynne had been

118

roared at for not keeping her straight, she tried again and this time jumped it easily.

"I never thought Stardust would take to it so quickly," Lesley told Alice as they dismounted and fed their ponies on handfuls of pony nuts and bread. And her warm glow of triumph was increased by the sight of her sister watching with a dismal face as piebald Chess stood stockstill at the end of the lunge rein and refused to move one step nearer the water.

"Do you know if he's ever been lunged?" asked David.

"Yes, I think so. We tried him out once at a pony club rally and he seemed to know all about it," answered Sarah.

"Great," said Julia. "I'll get him going first then." She took Chess away from the water and soon had him trotting round on the lunge rein and looking like a well-behaved pony. Then, gradually she moved the circle nearer the jump and still kept him going forward. It wasn't until she actually pointed him at the water that he stopped, and refused to budge.

"See if you can lead him forward, Sarah."

"He won't do it, I know he won't. It's just a waste of time," moaned Sarah, as Oliver tried to tempt Chess nearer with oats.

Julia gave the lunge rein to Lizzie and managed to persuade Chess to within a few strides of the water by tapping him on the hindquarters, but then he stuck again, and he still wasn't within dithering distance.

"Does he kick other ponies?" asked David.

"No, never."

"Good. Lesley, you ride Stardust alongside him. Better go on the hedge side. Sarah, you lead Chess and try to walk them both up to the edge of the jump."

Chess was persuaded to take another couple of steps, but then he stood rock-like again. Sarah was wailing that it was useless, and, except for those who were helping, everyone had lost interest and started to talk of other things. James was trying to dry his jodhs and socks by flapping them in the wind. Netti took one sock and waved it aloft on her whip.

"Lesley, go back a bit, take a short run then trot past Chess and pop over, O.K.? Sarah you keep Chess standing straight and make sure he watches."

Stardust popped over neatly and Chess, taken by surprise, moved forward without meaning to. Julia was tapping him with the whip again, Oliver was shaking the oats, David and Lizzie were making encouraging noises; he began to dither.

"Round again, Leslie," called David.

Stardust pushed past him and jumped over. "Go on boy!" everyone shouted, "Go on."

Suddenly Chess reared up, plunged into the water, knocking down the centre pole and waded out on the far side. Everyone cheered and he began to wolf down huge mouthfuls of oats as though they were his just reward.

"Keep some for next time, Ollie," said Julia, fishing in the water the the pole.

"And mind my plastic sheet. This is not a water splash but a jump," David told Chess, as Sarah and Lesley went back for a second try.

This time Chess jumped properly and made another greedy rush for the oats. Then they towed him over without Stardust, and finally Sarah mounted, and Stardust, Berry and Hobbit were all told to give him a lead and to go round twice without stopping.

Sarah hardly knew whether to be pleased that she had a pony which now jumped black plastic and water, or annoyed that David had proved her wrong, but Tina and Lynne were both so loud in praise of their ponies and of David's Irish method, that she didn't have to say anything at all.

David, who seemed suddenly anxious to get away, called for quiet. "That's all for today," he said, "and tomorrow I'm going to hospital for a check-up. I think all the ponies should have a rest; we've worked them quite hard. Would any of you like to do a very, very basic dressage test and go round the whole course individually on Friday?"

"A *dressage* test?" asked some voices in horror, but

others were already shouting, "Go round the whole course? Yes, *please*."

"Same time then," said David, climbing into the passenger seat of the Land Rover. "Will you drive, Julia? I'm whacked."

"Thank you!" the pony club members shouted after them. "Thank you, David. Thank you, Julia."

CHAPTER SEVEN

Clear The Course

On Friday morning, Alice and Hanif, trotting down the track from Four Cross, found Sarah waiting for them on the road.

"Hullo," she said. I thought I'd wait and tell you the news. My mother's determined to get a team to the Area Cup. She and Mrs Blacker were plotting all day yesterday and Julia agrees that we're good enough. They've got the rules and some copies of the dressage test and some new quiz books and they're all going to work on David today."

"Poor David," said Hanif. "I really do pity him. All this stupid fuss about teams."

"I hope everything was all right at the hospital and they didn't say we had been wearing him out too much. Has anyone heard?" asked Alice.

"Yes, Mummy telephoned to ask last night. He said they were pleased with him and said he was to carry on and do a bit more each day."

James was waiting for them at his gate. "I've got your clothes," he told Hanif. "My mother *would* wash and iron them. I kept telling her that I'd only worn them for two hours, but she's got a phobia about dirty socks. It's great about the team, isn't it Sarah? I read the whole of the Pony Club Manual last night, in case I have to go in for the Quiz, but I'd rather not. I'm not as good as the rest of you at answering questions. I'd rather do the other sections. Is Jennifer coming today?"

"Yes, I think so. But I don't think Mummy's dared to tell David yet."

They found Mrs Rooke already in the field at Coppice Hill, unloading biscuit tin dressage markers from her car, and making a cross and reluctant Oliver arrange them round the school.

"He's doing it all wrong," James pointed out immediately. "He's jumbled all the quarter markers up. K should be on this side. Ollie!" he shouted.

"Go and sort them out," said Mrs Rooke. "Here's a copy of the test. I've brought one for each of you, but of course only the team have to learn it by heart. David's going to have it commanded this morning."

The pony club members read their dressage tests through gloomily. "You and I will lose three points straight away for not having snaffles," Alice pointed out to Hanif.

"That's not many, look what I'll lose when Jupe refuses to halt."

"Oh dear, there's a serpentine," wailed Lizzie.

"Do we really have to?" asked Rupert, "I'll never remember all this."

"You don't have to remember it, it's going to be commanded," Lesley snapped at him. "Someone stands at A and shouts the next movement just before you get to the marker where it begins."

By the time David arrived, the prospective team members had arranged the arena properly; James had even paced out all the distances. But the people who had never ridden a test before had worked themselves into a panic and, without even answering his 'Good morning all', they crowded round him asking questions.

"Must we do it?"

"What happens if your pony won't stand?"

"How do you know where four metres from the centre line is, when there's no line?"

"There's no marker for G."

"How big is a twenty metre circle?"

"We're going to begin by schooling," David shouted them down. "Will you all walk round on the old track, outside the markers, please."

As soon as the ponies were going well and on the bit, David started practising the various movements in the test. As they trotted round, everyone was called in turn to trot down the centre line and halt at X. The boys saluted by taking off their caps, the girls by putting their reins in one hand, dropping the other at their sides and bowing in the direction of the imaginary judge. They rode at the ordinary trot, at the sitting trot. Individually they made the smaller serpentine, half-circling about three yards on either side of where the centre line would be if there was one. They cantered and circled, they changed the rein and went through all the movements again. They practised halting and saluting all round the school and then walking on a long rein.

"There you are," said Daivd as they walked round him. "There's nothing to panic about; there's nothing in the test, except the salute, which we haven't done every day this week. Any questions?"

"Is it true you can't wear a martingale?" asked Alice, who had been told to take hers off by Sarah.

"In competitions, yes," answered David. "And you're not allowed to carry a whip, and the use of voice loses you points, so you can't talk to your pony. But none of that applies this morning; we're having a rough and ready practice in a very rough and ready arena. By the way, though you can practise the various *parts* of a test as often as you like, riding the whole test straight through should be done very rarely. You don't want the pony to learn the test. If they do, they begin to 'anticipate' and start the movements before you tell them to. Now I'm going to be the judge and I want someone to command; we'll use the loudhailer. Here, you, Lizzie," he went on quickly as Mrs Rooke began to say what a fine voice Sarah had. "You have to watch the rider and call out the instructions well before the marker at which the movement begins. Will the people who've ridden in dressage tests before come first, please."

James had ridden in several so he agreed to go first. Netti and Sarah, who had been in junior teams, offered to go second and third. Alice said she'd go fourth, if no one else wanted to, and Hanif said he would follow Alice. Gradually everyone found a place in the order.

"It's going to take quite a time," David told them, "about

five minutes each, so the people who aren't going early should dismount and give their ponies a rest, then start warming up again about ten minutes before they're due in."

Lizzie was good at commanding and James seemed very efficient at riding the test. Everyone except Netti, who was preparing to go in next, watched admiringly as James and Ferdinand entered at a steady trot and halted squarely at X. James saluted elegantly, David bowed back—he had no hat to take off—and horse and rider moved off at a trot round the arena. They serpentined, they cantered, circled at the canter, trotted and then, changing the rein at the walk, rode the serpentine and the cantering movements again, going round to the right. Finally they trotted down the centre, halting this time at the non-existent letter G, which James found by looking out of the corner of his eye for M.

"Well done," said David. "That wasn't at all bad. Your transitions are your weak point. You started cantering late on both reins. Try giving the aids a bit earlier. And the transitions back to trot were rather unbalanced, you need to put his hindlegs under him with a half-halt before you actually slow down. Then you could do with a bit more impulsion in the serpentines. You're inclined to put him to sleep and aim at neatness, but I want to see impulsion, hindlegs really working, back swinging. You won't do your jumping any good if you put your horse to sleep when you're schooling. But, as I say, it wasn't too bad at all."

Netti was ready, and Lizzie commanded her sister to 'Enter at ordinary trot sitting or rising'. Tristram moved well and, like Ferdinand, he had a good head-carriage. Netti kept calm and was able to think ahead and so be accurate.

"Good," said David when she bowed at the end. "That was another nice one. Your serpentines have come on a lot, but you're still cantering too fast on the circles. Try to sit down more and use the half-halt to slow him up."

Chess was next. He was too small and sturdy, too short-striding and thick-necked, to perform an elegant test, but it was obedient and neat and Mrs Rooke clapped loudly as he came to the final halt. "Every movement carried out precisely at the marker, nothing slipshod there," she announced.

"She wasn't in the same class as James and Netti." Lesley's bitter voice was equally loud.

"Little ponies can't really be judged against the bigger ones," said David calmly. "We all know that short strides and lack of presence will tell against them in a real competition, but at home we judge people on how well they've done with a particular pony."

"Like tack inspections," suggested Lizzie, who hated quarrels. "In your own pony club it doesn't matter if your tack's ancient, it's just judged on cleaness, but if you go against other clubs you've got to have good tack as well."

"Exactly," said David. "Come on, Alice."

Alice, suddenly overcome with nerves, made a very wavering entrance until David called to her that she must look at a point over the judge's head and not down at X. She made a crooked halt and a very hurried bow.

"Take your time, there's no rush," David told her.

Gradually as they trotted round, she and Saffron settled down, and though the pony sometimes escaped from her in the transitions and came off the bit, everyone could see that when he was on the bit he was calm, supple and occasionally a look of grace and distinction came over him, which set him apart from the other ponies.

"He bends beautifully," remarked Lizzie, eyeing his serpentine enviously, "and his steps are much more spaced out than Chess's"

"Yes, he has good cadence and a lot of potential," agreed David.

Hanif, in a ferment of worry, had thoroughly upset Jupiter. Instead of riding in quietly, he had found himself engaged in a pitched battle over halting and standing. When Oliver, who had appointed himself collecting steward, called him in, Jupiter bounced round C and entered, swinging his quarters and fighting for his head. Hanif forced him to a halt, but he refused to stand and twirled round and round.

126

"What's the matter with you?" asked David. "Why are you getting uptight, Harry? You've been doing all these movements perfectly well for days and now you go and work the pair of you into this ridiculous state. Take him away and calm him down. Walk on a loose rein and relax. You can try again after Lesley. And stop thinking you've got to *prove* something"

"Lesley, you look ready. Can you come now?"

Stardust's performance was an eye-opener to the other pony members. They had all be too intent on schooling their own ponies to see how other people were progressing and it was only at jumping that they had sometimes had the opportunity to watch each other. Now to see the pretty part-bred Arab trot into the arena was a great surprise. She no longer looked depressed and overbent. No longer weighed down by the pelham, her head had come up, better feeding had put a sparkle into her eyes and more of a shine on her chestnut coat, schooling had brought her hindlegs under her and given her impulsion. She looked quite different and certainly the most distinguished of the performers so far. She had a very long, slow stride, her cadence at the trot was even more pronounced that Saffron's, she stayed on the bit, and Lesley, like Sarah, was very accurate about carrying out movements exactly at the markers.

"Well done," said David when she came to her final halt. "That was very good. Here, I've made you some notes, small criticisms. The general impression was very good. Your walk is still your weakest point, it lacks impulsion; you'll have to try and improve it out hacking."

"Now, has Harry calmed down?"

"Has Jupe calmed down, you mean."

"No I don't. Jupe didn't even know we were planning to do individual dressage tests until Harry went tense and indicated that there was something unpleasant ahead."

"Well, I've decided not to care. I'm not going to try at all."

"Great, let's get started."

Except for David, Alice and Lizzie, no one watched Hanif's performance, they were all too stunned by Stardust. Lynne, Netti and Tina had all rushed to pat the pony, who looked very pleased at the unaccustomed admiration.

"She may not be much good at cross-country, but she's absolutely brilliant at dressage," said Netti.

"Brilliant," agreed Lynne. "Even better than Sea King."

"Oh, far better than him. She's up to Cranford Vale standard," said Netti.

"And far far better than anyone I've seen at the riding school," added Tina.

"Thank you." Lesley dismounted. "I didn't think I liked dressage tests before, but now I think they're good fun, and Stardust enjoyed it too. I think she likes people watching her."

"Why didn't Mrs Rooke clap Lesley?" Oliver asked Paul in a loud and indignant voice. "She was streets better than Sarah."

In the arena Jupiter was still bouncing a bit, but the fact that Hanif had given up trying to make him perform the movements exactly at the markers was helping.

"Don't halt," called David as he came down the centre at the end. "Carry on round and go through the whole test again. Now you've a rough idea how long he's going to take to obey your relaxed aids, try giving them a bit earlier and see if that makes it more accurate. Don't fuss him, just experiment calmly."

After Hanif came Rupert, and his was a very different performance. Rosie drifted round vaguely and neither of them seemed to be bothering much about markers. But they kept calm; Rosie only left the arena once, and she managed to do every movement in her own time.

"What a mess, just like Rupert," complained Mrs Rooke.

"Well done," David told Rupert. "That wasn't a bad test for a youngster and you didn't try to get hold of her which was sensible. Keep going like that and you'll find she'll improve gradually."

128

Paul's test was neat and accurate, but Banjo, like Chess, didn't really use his hindlegs and his small pony stride was a disadvantage. Lynne and Berry started well but when it came to the canter, the roan pony went back to her old habit of trotting faster and faster. Lynne, shrieking with horror, lost her way and, despite Lizzie's firm commands, continued in a state of confusion for the rest of the test.

"Terrible," she shrieked cheerfully halting at X. "We were awful. Much the worst."

Hobbit followed her into the arena, a serious expression on his dark-brown Dartmoor dish-face. Tina, looking pale beneath her freckles and concentrating grimly, managed quite well until Hobbit went on the wrong leg and she stayed on it for the whole of the canter movement, including the circle.

"Did you realise you were on the wrong leg?" asked David when she halted. "Because you should have corrected it. Leading off on an incorrect leg loses you a few points, but carrying out a whole movement on it means that you haven't done what was asked for, and as there were two movements, you would have lost twenty points."

"Sorry," said Tina.

"Don't be, you're here to learn. It was a nice test otherwise."

Lizzie was the last to go. She had been riding in while Netti commanded Tina and as she trotted into the arena, the watchers realised that they were in for another surprise. Rajah wasn't light and elegant, he didn't have the poetical appearance of Stardust, but he was energetic and on the bit, his long stride was cadenced, his back swung and he was bending correctly on all his corners, serpentines and circles as he plodded round with pricked ears and a learned expression.

"Well done, Lizzie, you only looked down twice and the old horse has improved out of all recognition." David turned to address the others. "I hope you've all learned something by watching each other," he said. "It's quite interesting to see how some of the ponies have come on;

they've all improved, but some had more hidden potential than others."

"My word, yes," said Mrs Rooke in a cross voice. "It's certainly confused things."

"We have an hour and a half for lunch," said David. "So only small feeds please, or they won't feel like galloping round the cross-country this afternoon."

After lunch the Land Rover party left for Coppice Hill before the ponies. Mrs Roberts had joined Mrs Rooke and Oliver, and when the riders reached the field they found the mothers had been hard at work, helping Oliver drag poles and drums from the two unwanted hillside jumps and build a new fence in the valley. The slip rails had been strenthened with extra cross poles and made to look more formidable, but otherwise the course was as before.

"I have the plan here," said David, "if anyone wants to look at it. These poles and drums are the first fence, then slip rail, water, logpile, tree trunk, ditch, brush, angle, horizon, then the little downhill jump and the gateway into the lane. This is where you've got to be careful. If you do get out of control down the hill, circle and stop *before* jumping into the lane. The gateway jump must be taken slowly, O.K.? Then you canter along the lane, jump back into the field over the slip rails and the Land Rover will be the finish. It'll be parked between the ditch and the brush. Oliver will be the starter, Mrs Rooke will steward the gateway jump and Mrs Roberts the water."

"I've got the best position," interrupted Mrs Roberts, laughing merrily, "but I'll fish you out quick."

"If you have three refusals at a jump, go on to the next and we'll sort you out afterwards. Any questions?"

"Do circles count as refusals?" asked Sarah.

"Normally, yes, but today isn't a competition; there are no prizes to be won."

"Do you want us to go fast?" asked James.

"A fair hunting pace, as they say; that's a hand gallop or a fast canter. This is an experiment, you have to find out what pace suits your pony. If the small ones start too fast they won't have the puff to get over the water, much less up the hill. And as I have already said, the gateway jump must be taken slowly. Now, we'll leave James and Harry down here and the rest of you come up the hill with me; you'll get a better view of what's going on. Remember, starter, when the first pony comes down the hill you can start the next one, but never more than two ponies on the course at once. And if anyone is in trouble we all wave our red flags. Our white ones signal that all is well again."

"Don't worry, I'll keep things under control down here," said Oliver.

From their vantage point on the hill, the other pony club members watched James start. He jumped the first two easily and then made the long journey to the water at a good cross-country canter. They saw him half-halt before he reached the water and then sit down and ride.

"He didn't mean to go in again," commented David as Ferdinand made a careful jump and turned uphill for the logpile. It was then that two figures, one mounted and one on foot, appeared at the lane slip rails.

"Who the hell . . ." began David.

"It's Mrs Blacker and Jennifer," said Sarah. "They mentioned that they might come and watch."

"I thought she asked Mummy if she could join in," said Lesley maliciously.

David turned his attention back to James who, riding hard at the ditch, was obviously prepared to foil last-minute attempts to run out. As he landed safely everyone shouted encouraging remarks.

"Those idiots are still on the course," complained David. He picked up the loudhailer and, waiting until James was over the brush, he shouted, "Clear the course, please. Wave at them, will you, Lesley?" he asked, looking down angrily at his useless arm. "They don't seem to understand I'm yelling at *them*. They can't both be deaf."

Everyone began to wave, for James was over the horizon fence and heading for the downhill one at a steady canter.

At last Mrs Roberts realized what was wrong and ran across to the Blackers.

Below in the valley, Hanif started. James hopped neatly over the gateway jumps. Mrs Blacker stood arguing with Mrs Roberts in the middle of the course and Jennifer, unused to popping over jumps with short runs, refused the slip rails.

"*Clear the course!*" David gave an angry roar through the loudhailer. Hanif, who was coming fast because he had decided to let Jupiter have his own way over the easy jumps at the beginning of the course and then steady him down later, shouted too, scattering the mothers. James coming along the lane yelled indignantly at Jennifer to get out of his way. He pushed past her and jumped into the field as Hanif sailed confidently over the water. Jennifer took James's lead, jumped into the field and went to stand with her mother and Mrs Roberts.

"I hope Mum's giving them hell," said Paul as James came galloping up the hill to finish.

"Great," he said, dismounting and loosening Ferdinand's girths. "Really great."

"The course rode well, did it?" asked David, his eyes concentrating on Hanif, who trotted through the trees, popped over the angle jump, and then angled the horizon jump too, so that he didn't land pointing straight downhill.

Oliver started Alice. She was looking forward to her ride; she felt completely at home with Saffron now, and having jumped everything but the first jump, she had no qualms about the course. She was filled with happiness as she galloped along the valley; sailing over the jumps. She felt that Saffron was a partner; she was steadying him and sending him on, but he was agreeing with the arrangements, he wasn't having to be controlled.

Oliver started Rosie with encouraging shouts of "Go it, Dozey!" and was very disgruntled when she refused dead at the first jump. He longed for Rupert to be a hero brother and do well, but as usual it would be bossy old Netti who did the best of the Wheelers. "Oh go on, you stupid twit," he muttered angrily, and at the second try she did.

132

Rupert got going on the long gallop across the second field and Rosie jumped the water easily. She was suspicious of the logpile and made a large slow motion jump. After the tree trunk, Rupert slowed her up. "You've got to keep some breath for the ditch," he told her. She jumped it well, but then Rupert was so busy shouting and waving to the other pony club members that he almost ran out of the brush.

"Concentrate!" roared David after his departing figure. But he still managed to lose himself in the trees and had to circle before he could take the horizon fence.

"That's another refusal," said Sarah who was keeping the scores.

Lizzie started; she made certain that Rajah was alert and ready for a new jump. He jumped the first two easily and galloped on towards the water. When I'm over that I'll start to enjoy myself, thought Lizzie.

Rupert was having trouble at the gateway. He had forgotten to look the way he wanted to go, so Rosie had gone straight on and almost collapsed on her nose in the hedge across the lane, but Rupert sat tight and the pony recovered somehow.

"We're O.K., don't worry," Rupert shouted in reply to Mrs Rooke's inquiries, and, sorting themselves out, they galloped away.

Rajah had slowed to an obstinate refusal at the water. Lizzie, uncharacteristically severe, gave him a whack with her whip. "You've jumped it dozens of times, you're just being stupid," she told him crossly. At the second attempt he jumped it easily and thundered on, taking the logpile and tree trunk with no trouble at all.

"Old Ra's beginning to look like a cross-country horse," observed James, as the pony cleared the ditch and went on with pricked ears and a wise expression towards the brush.

"Except for Rosie, they've all looked good," said Alice, who was sitting on the ground with Saffron cropping the turf beside her.

"And she's coming home like a veteran," announced Hanif, as she appeared over the slip rails.

"The trouble is that nearly all the good people have gone; the disasters are about to start," said Lynne.

"There are still Netti and Paul to go," James pointed out. "They ought to go round clear."

"But now we have my sister, she's bound to make a mess of it," said Sarah as Lesley cantered along the valley. Stardust cleared the first two, but objected to jumping the water on her own and slowed to a suspicious halt. Lesley didn't start hitting and kicking: she let her have a look, gave her a pat and tried to sound confident as she said, "You'll do it easily." Then she took her away and got her going before she rode at it again. This time Stardust agreed to jump.

"Well done, dear," shrieked Mrs Roberts, as Lesley galloped on.

"Here's Lizzie coming home. She's done very well," said Tina.

"Lesley's being a bit slow over the downhill jumps, but she's doing them all," said Lynne. "Netti's starting. It's nearly time for us to go down."

Netti had complete confidence in Tristram, she knew that he would take her round; all she had to do was to sit tight and remember the course, he would do the rest. She loved jumping him and cross-country was her favourite, she thought, as she galloped over the fields, clearing jump after jump.

Paul was slower, but equally clear. He had to take the hill slowly because Banjo was clearly running out of breath, but he was very neat and quick over the angle jumps and in the gateway.

"He wouldn't be much use for racing, he jumps too big," said David, when Banjo had arrived, puffing, at the Land Rover. "All these huge stag-like jumps he makes take it out of him and slow him up. He's a Puissance horse by nature. He'd love to go on jumping one enormous fence all evening."

"Which of them would you choose for racing?" asked Hanif.

"Well, yours would be all right for the big fences, and

134

Saffron has the right ideas, but if I wanted a hurdler I'd take Rosie." Rupert began to express amazement that anyone should want Rosie for anything, but then Lynne, who had refused twice at the water, stopped again at the ditch.

"A *short* run!" roared David.

All the pony club members began to make encouraging noises and Berry went over at her second try. She cantered boldly at the brush and then trotted carefully over the angle, horizon and downhill jumps. Sarah and Chess set off along the valley and Tina waited all alone at the start. Her teeth were chattering and her legs were shaking. She had never ridden round a course before. She's never ridden in anything, not handy pony or even egg and spoon; she had never realised that you felt like this. It was awful.

Sarah hadn't approached the water with much confidence. She'd kicked for all she was worth and shouted, "Go on, Chess!" to hide her feelings, and for a brief second she thought he was going. But then he stopped, and she went on, very slowly, over his lowered head and into the water. She climbed out quickly and began to scream at Chess, telling him what a perfectly beastly and ghastly pony he was. "I hate you," she shrieked, stamping her foot angrily, while Mrs Roberts and Mrs Blacker tried to remove her dripping anorak.

"We'd better send down a lead," said David, looking round. "You go, Lesley, he'll follow his stable companion. Then, if she jumps it, let her go on alone."

Lesley didn't like to argue, so she went reluctantly, knowing that Sarah wouldn't be at all pleased to see her.

"Poor Tina," said Paul. "This'll put her right off. But look, here's Lynne. Come on Lynne, gallop."

"What do you want?" Sarah, whose anorak had been forcibly removed by Mrs Roberts, shouted at her sister.

"David says I'm to give you a lead. He says Chess will follow Stardust."

The sisters glared at each other angrily. "Oh, all right," said Sarah, remounting, "but I bet all that happens is that you refuse too."

Stardust didn't refuse, she jumped in fine style, and Chess followed her. Mrs Robert's cheer was echoed by the watchers on the hill. Sarah went on alone.

"Now Hobby, a clear round, please," said Oliver, patting his pony's neck. "Are you ready? On your marks. Go."

Tina's legs recovered before she reached the first fence and she forget her teeth. The slip rails loomed up, friendly and familiar, and the long canter to the water settled her and Hobbit down. She rode hard at the water, hoping to disguise a slight faint-heartedness, and Hobbit, with a small pony's cleverness, knew that she wasn't happy about it, and jumped the wing.

"Do I have to go back?" Tina shouted to Mrs Roberts.

"No, dear, you go on. That'll do," Mrs Roberts shouted back, for she believed in a comfortable life.

"It doesn't count. She'll be eliminated if she goes on," objected Jennifer.

"Oh goodness, it's only for a bit of fun, and I expect poor Tina was a bit put off by Sarah's splash. Well, that's the last one round then. They *have* done well. David must be pleased with them."

"No, Jennifer's going last," said Mrs Blacker. "Mrs Rooke says David won't mind. Go on, darling, down to the start. We mustn't keep everyone waiting."

Jennifer ignored Oliver, who told her she couldn't start until Tina was halfway down the hill. She simply rode through his flags and started. Muttering angrily, Oliver took down his flags and started up the hill, intending to complain to David.

Jennifer was riding down the valley at a slow canter, sitting in her saddle, and not looking in the least like a cross-country rider thought Hanif, who had watched her start. Tina had stopped at the ditch, mainly because Hobbit was out of breath. The Wheelers all made encouraging noises, but David said, "Don't hurry him, let him get his second wind."

As soon as he had got his breath, Hobbit went on will-

136

ingly and then shouts from the water drew everyone's attention to Jennifer. Sea King was dithering on the brink, Jennifer was shouting, both mothers shooing.

"I didn't know *she* was going round," said Lizzie as Sea King got over and turned up hill.

"Nor did I," said David in a cold, angry voice. "Well, she's nothing to do with us, so we'll go down and have all those who stopped at the water over again. Rupert, I think you should do the gateway jump properly."

The pony club members mounted. Jennifer seemed to be having trouble at the logpile. Oliver, puffing from his climb up the hill, stumped over to the Land Rover and complained, "That Jennifer Blacker wouldn't listen to me. She started herself, though I told her that she had to wait until Tina was down from the trees."

"Some people have no manners," David spoke quietly but his pale face was set in hard angry lines and his blue eyes flashed with annoyance. "But don't worry, I'll be having a word with Miss Blacker presently."

"I don't think David's very pleased at Jennifer turning up like this," said Lizzie in a worried voice.

"I'm sure he isn't. He looks absolutely furious," agreed Rupert.

"Oh dear, I hope he doesn't explode and spoil the last day, when it's all been so lovely," moaned Lizzie, who hated rows.

"You can't blame him. It is awful cheeck just turning up and going round without asking." Netti sounded indignant.

Jennifer was crashing about in the trees and cursing Sea King. The two older Wheelers, Alice, Hanif and Lesley stayed to watch. Everyone else was making for the water.

"Do you think we ought to help her?" asked Lizzie.

Sea King appeared suddenly, making a huge leap over the horizon fence, pecking and then setting off down hill at a canter.

"Whoa," yelled Jennifer, pulling him sideways, "Whoa."

"That looks dangerous."

137

"David gave a terrible roar when I tried going down sideways," said Alice, "He seemed to think that Saffy was about to cross his legs and fall."

Jennifer straightened up as she came to the downhill jump, but it was too late for Sea King to take off. He crashed through, scattering poles and drums, which rolled away down the hillside. Jennifer was round his neck, but she quickly regained her seat. She was going far too fast, but she seemed to decide to take a chance on the gateway jump.

"Circle!" shouted Hanif.

"She probably thinks that pole is all there is," said Lesley. Lizzie shut her eyes as the pony flung himself at the jump. There was a crack and a thud and the sound of splintering wood as pony and rider disappeared from sight. Without a word the five of them cantered down the hill. As they came to the gateway they could see the pony scrambling to his feet, pulling back to get free from the entangling hedge. The baling string holding the second pole had snapped. They slid carefully down into the lane.

"Are you all right, Jennifer?"

"No, of course I'm not. He fell on me and I'm all tangled up in this hedge."

Lizzie flung her reins to Rupert.

Sea King had obviously been going too fast to stop. He had hit the second pole, catapulted across the lane and crashed into the hedge with its strengthener of post and wire. Alice gave her reins to Hanif and ran to help Lizzie, who was clearing the chunks of broken thorn, splintered post and rusty wire, so that they could inspect Jennifer.

"Do you think you've broken anything?" asked Lizzie.

"How do I know? Where's King?" Jennifer sat up suddenly. "Haven't you got him? Well go and catch him, you fools."

"His bridle's here," said Alice, disentangling it from post and wire.

"The Land Rover's coming," announced Lesley in relieved tones, " and the mothers are there with David."

"Better get the ponies out of the way," said Lizzie.

"We're a bit redundant here. We'd better go after the pony," said Hanif as Mrs Blacker and Mrs Rooke emerged from the front of the Land Rover, and Mrs Roberts from the back. David foll... them slowly.

With Alice carrying Sea King's bridle, they set off at canter along the soft centre of the lane. Then they heard the thud of hoofs behind them and found Lesley cantering in pursuit.

"David sent me after you," she told them, when they slowed down and let her catch up. "He said you were too new to know the way or the Roberts's telephone number or anything, and that I'd better come and help."

"Great," said Hanif. "We're simply following hoofprints."

"And there's been nowhere for him to turn off so far," added Alice as they cantered on again.

The track wound upwards, round the side of Coppice Hill, and as the ponies began to puff they all slowed to a trot. They reached the ridge where the woods ended and looked out across the green humped Downs, which stretched away for miles until they met the distant line of the sky.

"I hope he doesn't get out there. We'll never catch him," observed Alice. The chalk track widened, became grassy and they cantered on again. There were no hoofprints to follow any more, except on occasionally muddy sections of the track and then there were dozens, leading in all directions.

They began to grow anxious.

"He wouldn't have come as far as this, would he?"

"We must have missed him."

"Could he have got into the woods?"

They came to a crossroads. Four white tracks met and then wheeled away over the green hills, into space and sky.

"Shall we each take a track and ride a short way along it, looking for signs?" suggested Alice.

"All right, for five minutes, and then turn back. We don't want to lose each other, it's pretty vast up here," said Hanif.

He and Alice took the tracks that led along the ridge in opposite directions. Lesley took the one that led straight ahead and down into a hollow. Soon, long before five minutes was up, she was shouting, "Harry! Alice!"

They heard her and turning their ponies galloped back. They couldn't take short cuts for the wide tracks were fenced. They met at the crossroads and trotted down the hard chalk of Lesley's track. She was waiting for them.

"Look, my eyes aren't much good, but surely that's him, down there by the farm?" Their eyes followed the direction of her pointing finger and they both saw a weary-looking pony plodding along a beaten chalk track which led to the farm buildings.

"Oh *poor* Sea King, he's looking for help and a stable," said Alice.

"I don't think we're going to have much trouble in catching him," added Hanif as they set off at a brisk trot. They rode down into the hollow and then along the farm lane. When they drew close to the plodding bay pony they walked and called his name.

"Sea King," they called, "King." He stopped and turned and whinnied. He made no difficulties when Alice dismounted and approached him with the bridle, in fact his sorrowful expression brightened a little.

"Poor old boy, he is feeling sorry for himself," said Hanif.

"I'm not surprised, look at that." Lesley pointed to a triangular gash in his chest. "It's still bleeding."

"And look at his legs," added Hanif in a shocked voice. "They're cut to pieces."

"Blood everywhere," agreed Alice, who, now that the bridle was on, had begun a thorough inspection. "But I can't see anything that's likely to prove fatal."

"And the blood's not gushing out in torrents," observed Hanif, who had crouched down to get a better look at the inside of Sea King's legs. "The chest's the worst wound."

"Yes, but I don't think it's deep. It's a sort of horrid flap," said Alice, taking a closer look. "Do you think we can walk him home?"

"It'll take ages. What do you think, Lesley?" asked Hanif.

"I think we should go on to the farm and telephone for a box—well, David's is only a cattle truck, but the Roberts's must be home by now and they could send it."

"That sounds sensible. Two of us had better telephone and one stay with King."

"One of the telephoners had better be Lesley, as she knows telephone numbers and where we are," said Alice.

"And the other had better be me, if you don't mind," said Hanif, "because if Saffron goes, Jupe will start his twirling and that won't be much fun for Sea King."

So Alice found herself waiting in the lane, holding two ponies with quite different ideas. Sea King wanted to stand with drooping head, resting his legs in turn until he was rescued, while Saffron was hungry and insisted on grazing the sweet spring grass along the verges of the lane. In the end, Alice took off Saffron's pelham, and attached one complete length of rein to his noseband, then, each time he ran out of grass, she persuaded the poor stiff invalid to walk a few steps nearer the farm. She occupied herself picking choice morsels of grass for King, because she knew that if she did nothing she would begin to think gloomy thoughts. The course was over, it had been lovely, but like all lovely things it had come to an end. Soon the holidays would end and Saffron would go back to Mr Crankshaw. That didn't bear thinking about. She picked more and more grass for King.

The farm seemed deserted. There was a house, but it was surrounded by piles of bricks and window frames. A concrete mixer stood idle. There were no curtains at the windows.

"Anyone about?" shouted Hanif, as they headed for the farm buildings. "Anyone at home." But silence reigned everywhere until they heard grunting coming from one huge building which looked more like a village hall than a pig-sty. The door was locked, but they found a window open and from their ponies' backs they were able to peer in.

141

Hundreds and hundreds of pigs stood in tiny pens, row upon row of tiny prisons. They were big pigs, it didn't look as though they could even turn round.

"It's horrible."

"And there's no one here."

"Someone must come to feed them."

"I expect it's done automatically. There's a sort of droning noise."

"Let's go, we're wasting our time."

"We'll have to walk him all the way home then," said Hanif.

"No, look, there's a way out to the road down there. I'll go on ahead," decided Lesley. "I'll hope to find a telephone, but if not I'll go all the way to Garland Farm and send them to meet you."

"But how do *we* know where to go?"

"There's only one road at this end of the Downs. You just follow the signpost to Kidlake."

"That's a long way round. Wouldn't it be better to go back the way we came?"

"That track's too rough for trailers and boxes. They always get stuck. I'll tell them you'll be on the road," she called back as she trotted through the farm gate.

It was a horrible journey. Poor Sea King had stiffened up while he was standing and could scarcely hobble along. They felt very mean forcing him to walk, but Hanif explained to him that they would never be found unless they reached the road. The movement seeemed to do him good and he gradually unstiffened, but he still looked very sorry for himself and walked with a hanging head.

Hanif was in a continual panic convinced that he had misunderstood Lesley's instructions, that they were on the wrong road and would shortly come to a signpost with no mention of Kidlake on it.

Alice pointed out that so far there had only been *one* road to take and that, anyway, David and the Roberts's must know the pig farm when they lived so near. Then she went back to consoling Sea King with encouraging words

142

and promises of horse boxes, vets, deep-bedded stables and bran mashes.

They had come at last to a signpost, which offered Coombe Lentworth, Kidlake or The Downs, and Hanif had just given a small cheer on seeing the telephone box from which Lesley must have telephoned, when a large cattle truck came slowly along the road.

"It's them!" shouted Alice.

Mr Roberts was driving, and Paul, Lynne and Sarah were sitting beside him. They jumped out as the box stopped and gathered round Sea King, giving cries of horror at his wounds.

"I'll turn the box before we load him," said Mr Roberts and drove on to the crossroads.

"Is Jennifer all right?" asked Alice.

"She doesn't seem too bad," answered Paul.

"Her arm hurts so her mother's taken her to hospital for a check-up," explained Sarah.

"Mum thought she was making a bit of a fuss," said Lynne. "Still, better to be safe than sorry."

"Let's get those headcollars on," said Mr Roberts, coming back. "Lynne, you take the Blacker pony. Paul, give me hand with this ramp. We'll load the fit ponies first, and put the partitions between them. Come on, Alice, let's have yours first."

Saffron and Jupiter seemed pleased at the idea of a lift and made no difficulties. Sea King hurried up the ramp after them, as though afraid of being left behind.

"He'll live," said Mr Roberts, looking at him critically.

"Poor Jupe must be starving, I only gave him half his feed at lunchtime," observed Hanif suddenly as they left the Downs and drove into Kidlake.

"Well, you can give him the rest in a minute," Sarah's voice was bossy. "David wants to see us all in his house before we go home. He's in a terrible mood. He really blew Mrs Blacker up. When he found that Jennifer wasn't seriously hurt, he got into the most terrible rage, and he was quite rude to Mummy, too."

"I don't blame him," said Alice.

"What does he want us for?" asked Hanif suspiciously.

"To tell us about the Area Cup, of course."

"Then he doesn't need me, I'm not going in any team," objected Hanif.

"Yes he does. He want you *all* in there as soon as you've settled your ponies," said Mr Roberts firmly.

"What about Lesley?" asked Alice as they bumped down the lane to Garland Farm.

"She should be here by now, if she found the short cut through the wood. Now get a move on, we want those ponies watered and fed and you indoors quickly."

"There's tea in David's kitchen," Lynne added encouragingly, "and Mum's made two huge cakes."

CHAPTER EIGHT

Dress Rehearsal

Though it had been modernized, David's kitchen had kept its old-fashioned look. Long and low-ceilinged, furnished with an old wooden dresser and table, it was now full of people. The wheelback chairs, the basket chairs and the window seats were all occupied. Handed mugs of tea and huges slices of cake by Mrs Roberts, Alice and Hanif joined Rupert and Oliver who were sitting on the floor, their backs against the dresser.

Alice waved to Lesley. "It was a good idea of yours," she said. "They came quite quickly. We'd only just reached the proper road, so it saved poor King several miles."

Mrs Rooke was counting heads. "Twelve," she announced triumphantly, and David, who was sitting in one of the basket chairs, said, "Right, I'll begin. First of all I'm sorry that our course ended in confusion. As you know, this was caused by the bad manners and stupidity of someone who shouldn't have been there; she had refused to attend on the two earlier days. And it's only by sheer luck that neither pony or rider were seriously hurt." He did not look at Mrs Rooke, who seemed busy, studying a sheaf of printed details.

"Now, you will all remember that when Mrs Rooke mentioned the Area Cup at the beginning of the holidays I refused to consider entering a team. Since then you've all worked so hard and improved so much, some of you almost miraculously so, that, yesterday, I changed my mind. Then, as it seemed rather a shame only to enter five of you and I knew it was going to be very difficult to decide which five, I spoke to the organizers and they've agreed to let us enter *two* teams, and also an individual should we have anyone left over. This means that you can all go."

Nearly everyone was pleased.

"Oh *good!*"

"Terrific."

"It'll be much more fun if we all go."

Only Rupert and Hanif took the news gloomily. Rupert put up his hand and asked, "Can I be the individual, because then I won't let anyone down?"

"I think it ought to be me," argued Hanif. "I hate being in teams and my dressage is terrible."

"No, me. I'm the least experienced of you all," said Tina. "I've never ridden in anything, not even a gymkhana event, in my whole life."

"Can Netti and I and Lynne go with James?" asked Sarah.

"Yes, Lynne's brilliant at turnout and the quiz," agreed Netti.

"But you'll need someone to take Jennifer's place," Mrs Rooke pointed out. "We must choose the best out of all the others to make up a really good A team."

"What on earth is Sarah doing in an A team?" asked Lesley disagreeably. "Half the people on the course are better than she is."

"Well at least I . . ." Sarah began to shriek an angry retort, but David sat up in his chair and interrupted her. "In this branch, the District Commissioner chooses the teams," he said in a very firm voice. He brandished a sheet of paper. "And I've been working on the possible combinations. First of all, as the individual has to compete in all four sections, it can't be Rupert. I don't feel that Rosie's dressage is up to a public performance at present. I think it should be Tina. She and Hobbit are both good all-rounders, and I agree with her view that she is the least experienced of you all. I don't propose to have an A and a B team. I haven't seen you ride in competitions so I don't know how you react under pressure. We'll just have two teams and you can call yourselves what you like. In one I've put Alice, Lizzie, Lesley, Harry and Rupert. Rupert will stand down for the dressage, Lesley for the cross-country. I don't think Stardust should be asked to go round a strange cross-country until she's developed more self-confidence. I don't know which members of the team should enter for the quiz or the turnout, perhaps you can tell me, or we can consult Julia." He paused for a moment.

"Now, in the other team we have James, Netti, Sarah, Lynne and Paul. I don't think Berry is going well enough for either the dressage or the cross-country, but as Lynne tells me she'll be quite happy to do the quiz and turnout that doesn't matter. Any comments?"

"I still think it would be better to try and pick one really good team," said James. "We want the Woodbury to win for a change and that's not going to happen if you divide us into two more or less equal lots."

"I'm not aiming to win this year," David answered. "This is more of a trial run, a school, and it'll be a better school if both teams are in with a chance. Now would you like to get into your groups and sort out the quiz and turnout. We've paper and biros here. Tina, you come and have a look at the rules."

"Which first?" asked Hanif, who had the paper and pen.

"Turnout," said Lesley. "Who has reasonable tack?"

"Harry's is lovely and mine's bearable," answered Alice.

"Mine's just about bearable, I suppose," Lesley went on, "and then we'd better have you Lizzie. At lease Ra will be well groomed."

Lizzie gave a moan of dismay. "My bridle's so ancient, you simply can't get it to look nice, and my stirrups are awful plated things and half the plating has come off."

"Well, they only count the marks of the best three," Alice reminded her soothingly.

"Quiz?" asked Hanif.

"Not me," said Rupert. "I have absolutely no idea how many pounds of hay a pony should eat, or how many nails there are in a shoe."

"But you must be in something else," Hanif told him. "You can't just go in the cross-country."

"I don't see why not. If I survive that I shall have done my

147

duty for the honour of the Woodbury pony club," argued Rupert.

"Oh, wait a minute. If Rosie had Ra's saddle with my leathers and girth, but your irons, we could make up quite a respectable set of tack," said Lizzie. "Then you could be in the turnout and that would make two things."

"Turnout?" Rupert's face was full of horror. "But you know I'm hopeless at grooming and tack cleaning."

"I'll help you and so will Ollie," said Lizzie. "Don't you think that's a good idea?" she appealed to her other team mates.

"So Alice and I go in everything. Lizzie's not in the turnout, Rupert's not in the quiz or the dressage, and Lesley's not in the cross-country," announced Hanif, reading from his list. "Is that settled? Shall I give this to David? I must say I think it's crazy putting me in the dressage. I'm just as bad as Rupert."

"Only three scores count," Alice reminded him.

"I'll have a nice restful day," said Rupert contentedly.

"No you won't, you'll have to help the rest of us," Lesley told him. "Holding ponies, tying on numbers, fetching and carrying."

As David studied Hanif's list, Mrs Rooke read it over his shoulder.

"If Lesley's not going in the cross-country, why not try Sarah on Stardust?" she suggested, "She's a really game little rider. I'm sure she'd get the pony round and then we wouldn't have the problem of Chess and black plastic."

"No, they won't let them ride more than one pony, and anyway Stardust is really going well, her dressage is good. We don't want to upset her with a change of rider." Mrs Rooke was silenced.

"Come on, James, where's your list?" David went on. "I've promised to telephone the secretary with names before seven."

"Our list's easy, we've done that," answered James, handing it over. "I'm not going in the quiz, Paul's not going n the turnout, and Lynne's out of the other two. It's a name for the team that's holding us up."

"Woodbury Wonders," shouted Sarah. "It must be, James."

"Yes, come on, James," agreed the rest of the team.

"It doesn't matter, names are only for fun," David told them. "Now, tomorrow's a day off. All the ponies and I suspect, most of the riders, need a rest. Then on Sunday I want to do some *real* water. I'll fix it up with Mr Crankshaw over at Waterford farm—we'll splash about in the ford. We also need a flat field to do the test once more and I'm hoping he may be able to provide that too."

Alice looked at Hanif. "Your arena's lovely," she said, "all marked out and everything, and very near Waterford farm if you go through the woods."

"Yes, it's not bad." Hanif sounded doubtful.

"Would your stepfather mind eleven pones?" asked David. "We are rather an invasion."

"I don't know, shall I ask and ring you up?" suggested Hanif.

"We'll have to think about transport too," said David in a suddenly exhausted voice.

"You have a rest and think about that tomorrow," said Mrs Roberts, beginning to wash up the mugs piled on the sink.

Everyone was talking again. Mrs Rooke clapped her hands. "Time to go home," she announced. "Sunday morning, ten o'clock, just inside the Waterford Farm gate. We'll let you know if there's any change."

"Thank you, David," they said, crowding round him. "The cross-country was lovely."

"Really terrific."

"It was the most exciting day I've ever had."

Lizzie offered her services to Mrs Roberts, "Can I help you wash up?"

"No, I think it would be better if you got off home," said Mrs Roberts, looking anxiously at David. "I think he's in pain so the sooner we leave him alone for a bit of peace the better. See if you can get them moving dear."

"If they're going to be The Wonders, supposing we're the Washouts?" Rupert suggested to Hanif. "We don't want to compete."

"I do," said Lesley fiercely as they left David's house. "I'd love to show my mother that her little darling isn't such a wonder after all."

"Yes, let's be The Washouts," said Lizzie. "It's much better to sound useless and then do well, than the other way round."

Saturday wasn't much of a rest for the humans. Aunt Margaret had gone to a dog show so Alice decided to walk into Woodbury with her stirrup leathers and two keepers that were flapping on her bridle, and persuade the shoe mender to stitch them up while she waited.

Hanif, who hadn't told his parents much about the course and had been very careful never to mention the Area Cup, found himself compelled to ask if it would be all right for eleven people to use the dressage arena on Sunday and, while he was in the middle of explaining that David would be in charge, Lesley telephoned and said. "Look, we've got to have a quiz practice if we're not to make complete fools of ourselves. The "Wonders" are having theirs here, and anyway, the Wheelers have persuaded Julia to pull Rosie's mane and tail, so they want us to go over there. Alice's Aunt Margaret is at a dog show and my mother wants to coach Sarah's lot, so do you think your parents could do something?"

"I don't know, I'll ask," answered Hanif. "How many people need collecting?"

"You, me and Alice," snapped Lesley impatiently.

"What on earth was all that about?" asked Mr Franklin.

"I'm afraid it's another request—transport this time," explained Hanif. "It's this team thing I'm in. They want to have a quiz session over at Kidlake and no one has any transport."

"A team?" Mr Franklin's face lit up. "You never told us this was in the offing."

"I didn't know until last night. We thought that at the most there'd be one team, but now David's decided to send two."

"Well of course we must get you to this practice. We can't have you letting the side down. What time do they want their transport?"

Hanif checked with Lesley, who said that if they could be there at about two, Julia would stay and do the quizzing.

Hanif was overcome with gratitude when his stepfather insisted on changing his plans and arranging for a golfing friend to collect *him* so that Mrs Franklin could have the car for the pony club use, but he was less pleased when he had to explain precisely what he would be doing and the exact purpose of the Area Cup.

"You mean that you will be performing in all four sections, and that some of the others will only be in two or three?" asked Mr Franklin, beginning to glow with pride."

"Yes, but I'm not much good at dressage. I hope they won't have to count my score. Anyway, can I ring David and tell him that we can use our field tomorrow."

"Both teams are coming, that'll be quite a crowd." Mr Franklin sounded pleased. "I think I'll telephone your Mr Lumley myself; make sure I know exactly what he wants. I seem to remember putting down white lines at pony club camp. Do you have a copy of the test with the exact measurements?"

The Wheelers were in rather a state about Julia's visit. They all agreed that the saddle room must be tidied up in her honour and Netti said that they must also weed the yard.

Leaving the yard to the others, Lizzie threw out enormous numbers of ancient rags, old saddle soap tins, gruesome-looking bottles, which had long lost their labels and lengths of rotting rope. Then she swept out several inches of dirt, dust, dead leaves and cobwebs and cleaned the window so that there was far more light. By the time she had put the tack back on its brackets and the halters on their hooks she was worn out, but justly proud of her

151

efforts. She emerged into the sunlight to see how the others were doing. Oliver's broom lay abandoned and there was no sign of him. Netti had weeded two square yards of the cobblestones, producing a huge pile of grass, groundsel and dandelions, but the cleared space made the rest of the stableyard look much worse in comparison. Rupert had found a pot of blue paint and was dreamingly painting Rosie's stable door.

"Oh Netti, do stop weeding and take those weeds to the bonfire," wailed Lizzie. "Julia will be here in ten minutes and it all looks so awful. Rupert, it's no use starting to paint, the ponies will get wet paint all over them, and we *must* start grooming and tack cleaning for Tuesday."

But everything turned out much better than Lizzie expected. Mrs Wheeler had cooked a delicious lunch. Mr Wheeler was in a good mood and opened two bottles of wine. Julia, who was doing design at college, was able to talk about illustrating with Mrs Wheeler and architecture with Mr Wheeler so there were no long pauses or awful silences.

The arrival of Mrs Franklin driving Hanif, Alice, Lesley and Tina, who had decided that as Hobbit was a Wheeler she'd better join the Washout's practice, broke up the luncheon party. Netti departed on a creaking bicycle to the Robertses, who had agreed to give her a lift to the Rookes. Julia carried an armful of books and a folder of questions out to the saddle room.

"Supposing we talk about horsey things in general while I pull the mane and tail," suggested Julia, "and then I'll try the quiz questions on you afterwards. I don't think they'll be terribly difficult ones as the whole point of the Area Cup is to encourage the people who don't get into teams normally."

"Us, in fact," said Rupert, putting a halter on Rosie, who had been moved into Tristam's box to avoid the wet paint.

"The Wonders know all the quiz book answers by heart. Do you think we ought to get hold of some copies and learn them too?" asked Alice.

"Obviously, the more you know the better, but I think the setters of questions will probably try to think up one or two original ones."

With Oliver, Tina and Rupert as well as the four who were in the quiz team packed into the loosebox, it was a tremendous squash, but Lizzie sat in the manger and Oliver and Hanif and Alice astride the partition. Lesley said she must stand beside Julia as she wanted to watch, and then she would pull Stardust's mane herself.

"Initials," said Julia. "Someone is bound to get 'what do these initials stand for? BHS. BSJA. BFSS. NH. RSPCA!"

They all shouted out the answers at once. British Field Sports Society was the only one no one knew. They went through the name of the Chairman of the pony club, the whereabouts of its headquarters, and the names of their own district commissioner and secretary. They listed the names of the grooming tools, the names of the tools used in shoeing and what they all looked like and were used for. They went through the markings a pony could possess, from races and blazes to eel stripes and ermine marks. Then points of the horse from ergots and chestnuts to stifles and gaskins and hamstrings. By the time Rosie's mane was pulled, most peoples' heads were reeling with the weight of so much knowledge. Rosie seemed to enjoy the mane part, but when it came to pulling her tail her co-operation ceased. She kicked out angrily and Rupert had to try to divert her attention with pony nuts and conversation, while Julia, standing well to one side, pulled away at the tail hairs.

Afterwards they all sat on upturned buckets in the yard and Julia went through her list of questions, quizzing everyone in turn. Lesley and Tina were the best on stable management, but Alice knew most about foreign breeds and was good on horses in history and in books. Hanif was very vague on questions about how many pounds of hay or nuts or anything else should be given to his pony—he always answered in scoops and haynets, which Julia said was useless—but he knew what FEI stood for and he was a lot better than Rupert. No one knew much about racing and Julia said they must memorize the names of the classic races. The fact that the Derby was for three-year-old colts and was run at Epsom. The Oaks was for fillies. The names of the horses who had last won these races and, of course, the Grand National. "There's bound to be at least one question on racing," she said as she handed out books.

"Thank you," they shouted after her as she mounted her moped and rode away. "Thank you, Julia. Thank you very much."

"Look at Rosie," said Rupert, leading her out into the yard. "Doesn't she look *civilized*. No longer a country bumpkin, but a slick show pony."

"That's going too far," objected Lesley. "But she does look a lot better."

They met at Waterford Farm on Sunday morning and found themselves lined up in a water meadow and minutely inspected. Julia advised on manes and tails and even snipped at a few on the spot. The rules of the competition banned plaiting, so there was no way of disguising messy manes. David inspected the tack and grooming. Several people were told to polish up their buckles, and to get the grease off saddle flaps or the inside of their reins while dusty rumps and muddy briskets abounded.

Chess was found to have a risen clench, which would go against him in the turnout, but Mrs Rooke said she would send for the blacksmith first thing on Monday morning.

David grumbled about muddy and unpolished boots and Mrs Rooke threw both teams into confusion by asking about riding jackets and gloves. "Polo necks for the cross-country, white shirts and pony club ties for the quiz, riding jackets for the dressage and the turnout," she announced firmly.

"But I'm only an individual," objected Tina. "Won't my anorak do?"

"I've outgrown my jacket. Lizzie's got it," protested Rupert. "Can't I wear my polo neck for the turnout too?"

"My jacket will do for the turnout, but as it's miles too small I can't possibly wear it for dressage," added Alice.

"Honestly, Mrs Rooke, I can't move my arms in it, and Aunt Margaret's in no mood to buy me another."

"We could pass jackets round for the dressage," suggested Hanif, who owned everything, even gloves. "You can have mine, Alice, but that's no good for turnout if we all go in together."

"Now let me deal with this, Harry," said Mrs Rooke sharply. "When I've made a note of what everyone needs I will go home and see what we have in our secondhand shop. Netti, your boots are all to pieces. I'd better see what I can find for you. Lizzie's crash cap is green with age. I'll make a note of your size. Alice, if there's a jacket to fit you, you can swop it for your old one, so your aunt won't have to worry about the expense, and I'm sure there's one that Tina can borrow just for the day."

"Now we're going to do everything the wrong way round." said David when the inspection was over. "We're going to do our jumping and messing about in the river *before* we go on to Harry's field for dressage. It's not a procedure I'd recommend, it's just convenient this morning. Alice and Harry, can you lead the way through the ford, please."

The river caused very little trouble. Saffron and Jupiter knew it so well that they were prepared to go backwards and forwards, encouraging the other ponies, and few made any fuss. Ferdinand insisted on trotting across at a very high cadenced trot which splashed everyone. Stardust teetered on the brink timidly and then decided to follow the others. Chess said he didn't mind *water,* it was black plastic he couldn't stand, and Berry caused the only uproar by trying to lie down. However, Paul raced to his sister's rescue and walloped Berry on the quarters until she changed her mind.

When all the ponies were splashing about happily and obviously enjoying themselves, Julia, assisted by James, who seemed to be the only rider with non-leaking boots, placed the two cavaletti David had brought on either bank so that whichever direction you came from, you jumped the first one into the water and the second one out on to dry land. The ponies, who knew now that the water was shallow and the bottom hard gravel, all enjoyed this too. "Right," said David. "Harry's going to guide you through the woods to his house. I'm going round by the road. See you there."

Mr Franklin had worked on the dressage arena until darkness fell on Saturday night. The pony club members were suitably impressed. They admired the white lines round the outside and up the centre and the fact that they now had an X at which to halt. James paced out the distances and announced that they were absolutely correct. But it was Hanif's jumps they really envied.

"Six real showjumps," said Netti. "Oh, Harry, you are lucky. Do you think David will let us jump them?"

"No. My stepfather suggested it, but David said we'd got to concentrate on dressage today. You'll all have to come again another day and try them."

"The arena's exactly what we need though," said James, looking pleased. "It'll give us a really good dress rehearsal. Double our chances of doing well."

"Please note that it belongs to a Woodbury Washout who is sharing it willingly with the Wonders," announced Rupert loudly. "*We* do not have the dog-in-the-manger attitude that is sometimes noticeable among members of other teams."

"What's been going on then?" Alice asked Lizzie.

"Oh, it's mostly Sarah. She didn't want Netti to let me use her quiz book. She seems to want to beat us more than all the other pony clubs."

"We'll have the people who live a long way off first," announced David as soon as he had parked the Land Rover at C. "That means that Harry, Alice and the Rookes can water and feed their ponies now. We won't want them until this afternoon. Now, no whips, martingales or voices, please. We'll have James first as he looks as though he's been riding in. Julia, will you come and write for me? I brought some dressage sheets so that we can give them my comments to digest."

The dressage was rather dull and took ages because David sent people back for coming in crooked and made them repeat unbalanced transitions, over-large circles and shapeless serpentines until they got them right. The pony club members drifted away to try on the collection of jackets, boots, caps and even gloves that Mrs Rooke had produced.

Alice was delighted with her riding jacket and wanted to go home and fetch her old one at once, to cement the swop. The only one which fitted Tina was a rather revolting ginger colour, which didn't go well with her reddish hair, but everyone agreed that when she had her crash cap on it made her look very smart. And they all felt that they looked much better riders when they wore jackets instead of anoraks.

Hanif was horrified when at lunch time his mother carried out a dish of Samoosas to the Land Rover and his stepfather followed her, bearing an assortment of drinks. But David seemed very cheerful and pleased with everything. He congratulated Mr Franklin on the dressage arena and Mrs Franklin on her cooking, and Julia said that the pony club had become much more fun for the junior instructors since Mrs Smythe gave up being D.C.

CHAPTER NINE

We'll Persuade Them Somehow

"It all seems very highly organized," Hanif told the occupants of the Garland Farm cattle truck as they led their ponies down the ramp. "Alice and I got here first of the Woodburys, the posh horsebox arrived a few minutes ago and there's still no sign of James. My stepfather and Julia have gone to get the numbers and find out if the programme is running to time. You've never seen so many highly-polished ponies in your life."

"What are the jumps like?" asked Rupert.

"I don't know. The cross-country's miles away. You can't see any of it from here."

"The turnout's being judged in the farmyard and the quiz in the house," said Alice. "The dressage has just started and it's in that field over there."

"Ollie, can you find the water brush? Rosie's sat on her tail and completely ruined it in spite of the tail bandage," wailed Lizzie.

"Here you are, but I'm helping Tina," Oliver replied ungraciously and hurried away to the hired horsebox which had brought Netti, Tina and the Rookes.

"Rupert, do come and help," wailed Lizzie.

"What with?" asked Rupert. "You're dealing with the tail and the rest of her looks perfect."

"You could give the tack a final polish or pick out her hoofs."

"You polished the tack the whole way over here. It *can't* need any more polishing. And her hoofs have been oiled so, if I pick them out, you'll be screaming at me for having an oily white shirt."

"Oh dear, I forgot they'd need picking out after the horsebox."

158

"I'll do it," offered Paul. "I'm not in the turnout and I haven't changed yet."

"James has arrived," announced Hanif, "so all the riders are here. Only David's missing."

"Mrs Rooke's driving him. As he's not really needed for the turnout and quiz she was planning to start a bit late," explained Paul. "Mum and Dad reckon the dressage and cross-country will be quite enough for someone in his state."

"The cardboard ones are to be worn on the backs for turnout, quiz and dressage," said Mr Franklin, handing out numbers. "There are real cross-country ones for this afternoon and they'll be in the back of the car."

Julia appeared. "'For the turnout, the ponies are to be tacked-up, but they're shown dismounted. You lead them in, stirrups run up, reins over the head. It's all running to time at the moment, so would the humans get dressed, please. Don't forget your crash caps and gloves.

"Rupert, your shirt's hanging out and your tie's crooked," snapped Lesley as the Washout team assembled.

"Here, you tuck the shirt in, I'll deal with the tie," said Mr Roberts, who had just finished brushing and polishing Lynne.

"I think we all look incredibly smart," said Hanif, looking round.

"Almost unrecognisable," agreed Alice. "Look at James! I don't know whether his boots or Ferdie's coat shine the most."

"Some of Chess's white bits are still sticky," moaned Sarah.

"You and Berry look perfect, absolutely brilliant," Netti told Lynne. "If only Sarah or I were as good as you and James we'd be bound to win."

"One of the team that's being judged now has a risen clench," Oliver reported with pleasure.

"But have you seen that team over by the scoreboard?" asked Tina. "They've got *black* jackets and *buttonholes*."

"*Too* got up," said Julia firmly. "They don't look like

159

pony club members. Come on! The collecting steward is waving at us."

The turnout judges were very thorough and very slow. One judge inspected the pony, a second the tack, while the third peered critically at the riders. Then they all wrote their marks on efficient-looking forms attached to clipboards before moving on to the next pony. It was very dull standing in line and waiting for them. The ponies became restive and would rub their spotless bridles against their elegant owners, who became bad-tempered and afflicted with aching legs.

The Woodbury Wonders were inspected first, and as soon as the ordeal was over they hurried out, talking excitedly.

"All three judges said 'Excellent'," James told his mother. "But I couldn't see what marks they were writing down."

"I was told I'd left saddle soap in my noseband buckle," observed Netti ruefully, "and the grooming judge made tiresome noises about Tristam's brisket. I really had body-brushed it for hours."

"They said I was 'Excellent' too." Lynne was all smiles. "The tack judge said I had kept my saddle beautifully."

Sarah wasn't so happy. "One of them said I ought to have scrubbed Chess's white bits harder and the other one complained my reins were stiff. I thought they were beastly judges."

"Look, will you tie the ponies up and start thinking about the quiz," ordered Julia. "They want you at the house as soon as you can make it. You're going against the South Barset team and they've done their turnout."

"Are the Washouts against the ghastly team with black coats and fancy browbands?" asked Oliver. "They're next in the turnout."

"I expect so."

Mr Roberts and Mrs Morgan chivvied the the Wonders back to the horseboxes, while Mr Franklin and Julia waited for the Washouts, who came out of the judging area giggling.

"They said the Woodbury had some exceptionally good boys," explained Rupert. "I nearly said it was all Lizzie and Mrs Morgan and that only Harry actually did any work, but I managed to control myself. What did they say to you, Alice?"

"Oh, they asked if Saffy was Connemara and if he was my own. They seemed quite pleased, but they didn't go into raptures."

"The tack judge talked to me very slowly; she thought I didn't understand English," said Hanif in an offended voice, "but she admired my saddle. What about you, Lesley?"

"One of them asked me if Stardust was part-bred Arab. Silly question; it's obvious, isn't it? I don't think they were terribly impressed by my tack."

"Well, put the ponies away and get ready for the quiz," said Julia. "I'll go in with the first lot."

Though James wasn't in the quiz, he had collected his team together and led them towards the house, making encouraging remarks in an attempt to keep up their spirits.

"The South Barsets look very old and brainy. They'll beat us easily," moaned Netti.

"Nonsense, you girls are all brilliant, you know *everything*," James told her firmly.

The quiz didn't seem to take nearly as long as the turn-out, and by the time the Washouts had swopped bridles for headcollars, tied their ponies to horseboxes and the trailer, taken off their jackets, caps and gloves, tied on each others numbers and wandered over to the house, The Wonders were emerging.

"What was it like?"

"How did you do?"

"Where the questions hideous?" they all asked at once.

"They were terribly good, quite as brainy as they looked."

"Yes, they were brilliant. They knew who wrote the books about Mr Jorrocks, which we didn't," added Netti.

"We lost by two marks and one was my fault I forgot the St Leger," said Lynne sadly.

161

"It doesn't matter whether you win or lose, it's your *score* which counts," Julia told her, "and you clocked up a high one compared with some of the earlier teams. You all did very well."

"I got the question about blacksmiths' tools," said Paul, who was looking quite pleased with himself.

"Wonders, go and tack-up for dressage," ordered Julia. "And The Washouts had better come in and get their bearings. I can see the Frogmorton lot approaching."

The two teams filed into the dining room of the farmhouse and took their seats at opposite ends of the table. The question master and scorer were sitting in the centre of one side, and, facing them, the audience on rows of chairs, filled the rest of the room.

Hanif was pleased to see that the Frogmorton team, still wearing black coats and buttonholes, looked very young and nervous and were shaking worse than he was.

The question master, who was fat, red-faced and jolly, seemed to be trying hard to put the contestants at their ease. He made a lot of jokes as he announced the teams and explained the rules. Then they were off. Lesley had the first question. It was on the correct fitting of the saddle and seemed suspiciously easy, but she answered it well. Then Alice was asked about martingales, Hanif about the aids and position of the pony when circling, and Lizzie to explain the natural and artificial aids.

The Frogmortons were less certain over the fitting of the bridle; they were good at bits, but confused about the halt and forgot several reasons why a pony might refuse. So it went on, questions about feeding and points of the horse, questions on lameness and first aid. Questions on racing and horse trials, polo and show-jumping, questions on horsey writers and painters. They had no time to think how they were doing, they were completely absorbed with question and answer, or waiting, lynx-like, to pounce on anything unanswered by the other side.

When it was over and they burst out into the sunshine again, they found David, Mrs Rooke, most of the parents and the mounted Wonders all waiting to hear how they had done.

"We weren't bad," said Lesley. "We managed to answer one or two of their questions which may be a help."

"We did *much* better than I expected," added Lizzie.

"Lizzie knew all about horsey painters," said Oliver with pride.

"And Harry answered a horrible question on polo, which the girl on the other side had to pass."

"Which of our teams has done best so far?" asked Sarah.

"The Wonders did best in the turnout, the Washouts in the quiz," Julia answered.

"But the dressage carries more weight than either of them, so let's start riding in," said David. "Come and find me in the collecting ring as soon as you're ready. Harry, will you ride round and round the horsebox park at the walk and trot, just exercising and keeping Jupiter very calm, until I send someone to fetch you. Don't start practising bits of the test or you'll upset him."

Mr Franklin had already tacked up Jupiter, and, carrying Hanif's crash cap, was coming to meet them. When he had seen Hanif off on his first circuit of the horsebox park, he helped Alice with Saffron, which was just as well for her hands had suddenly become weak and unable to pull up girths or fasten buckles. It was worse when she was mounted, for her legs had become weak too, and an excited Saffron, stiff-backed and star-gazing, jogged over to David.

"It's having no martingale," wailed Alice.

"You managed without one on Sunday," David reminded her. "Calm down, put him on a circle and don't trot until you've got his head down at the walk. I'll sort you out as soon as I've got the first four going."

James, looking solid, straight and not at all nervous, was riding round outside the arena, waiting to be called in. As the judge, sitting in a car at C, honked the horn, James broke into a steady trot and entered at A.

"I can't bear to look," said Mrs Morgan, who seemed

163

much more nervous than James. "Tell me how he's doing, Alice."

Alice watched as she circled. "A good halt," she said, "and he's standing there for hours, making sure the judge has noticed. Now he's proceeding at a nice steady trot. He's remembered to sit. The first loop of his serpentine looks a bit flat to me. The second one's better, and the third. He cantered a bit late, but it was a very smooth transition and he's on the right leg. I think you can look, Mrs Morgan, he's doing very well."

"Well done, that was good," said David, as James came out, patting Ferdinand and looking pleased.

"Good luck, Netti," shouted the Woodbury supporters as she rode into the roped enclosure and began to walk round.

"Go and see how Harry's doing. I'll want both of you over here in about five to ten minutes," David told Alice as Mrs Rooke came hurrying towards him with the urgent look of a sheep that has lost its lamb.

"David, Chess is having an attack of temperament. He suddenly refuses to stand. I don't know what can have got into him. He's never behaved like this before, and the poor child's working herself up into a state."

"Send them over here," said David calmly. "Yes, Paul, what's the matter with you?"

"I've forgotten the test and lost my copy," announced Paul in a voice of quiet despair.

"Well, cheer up and watch Netti, she's just beginning. Now, Sarah, what's your trouble?"

"He keeps swinging his quarters about and he won't stand."

"Well, calm yourself down, hold the reins in one hand and pat his neck. If the rider gets tensed up she's bound to affect her pony."

"Yes, I know. I wish you'd tell Mummy to go away, she's making me worse."

Alice found Hanif cowering behind a very large horse-box.

"I'm hiding from my stepfather," he explained. "He's

164

found the scoreboard and worked out exactly how many marks the Washouts need to take the lead."

"What a waste of time," said Alice briskly. "I heard David telling Mrs Rooke that everything depended on the cross-country. It's got a possible total of two hundred marks."

"Yes, you're right *and* it's possible to get them all too," said Hanif, cheering up. "No one ever gets a hundred per cent for dressage, do they?"

"I suppose Olympic gold medallists might, but no one else. Let's go over there and school near Lizzie and Lesley. They're halfway to the collecting ring."

Lizzie and Rajah seemed to be going very well in their steady, plodding way.

"Ra seems to go better when he's a bit excited," Lizzie told them happily. "It gives him more impulsion. Did you see how Netti was doing?"

"No, David sent me away just as she was starting. We ought to trot round a bit, Harry. Come on, let's circle."

Lesley rode across to the arena feeling quite surprised at her own confidence and calmness. She was glad that she didn't have to go in the cross-country. She knew that she'd only have made a fool of herself and given her mother and Sarah a chance to crow, but she was actually looking forward to the dressage and she knew that Stardust was going to enjoy it too.

"Don't try and do the best test of your life," said David when she joined him in the collecting ring. "Just aim for a reasonably good one. She's going beautifully. Her carriage and cadence are improving every day."

"How have the others done?" asked Lesley, who wasn't used to compliments.

"Not badly. James and Netti were good. Sarah started badly, but did quite a neat test once she settled. Paul forgot his, but the judge sorted him out. He won't have lost too many marks."

They watched Paul halt neatly at the end of his test. "Right, he's finished," said David. "Now, you know what

165

to do? Walk round outside the arena until she's ready. The judge will toot the car horn at you."

Paul, shamefaced, tried to creep away unnoticed, but David called him over. "That wasn't at all bad for your first try in public," he told him. "Plenty of people forget their tests. The great thing is to keep your head and not go completely to pieces. You won't have lost many marks."

Alice, Hanif and Lizzie had all arrived in the collecting ring and were trying to watch Lesley while riding their ponies in. Mrs Roberts handed round barley sugar and made comforting noises. David made Alice and Hanif trot circles, but seemed to be watching Lesley most of the time.

Stardust seemed pleased to be in the arena, showing off her paces to a judge without the bother of keeping up with a ride, or the worry of jumps. She halted elegantly, head high, neck arched and on the bit and then trotted on with a cadence that none of the other Woodbury ponies possessed. Her serpentines flowed, fluent and supple, her canter was slow but full of impulsion, her ears were pricked and her expression contented throughout.

David looked more and more pleased as the test went on, and Mrs Rooke and Sarah, standing beside him, were obviously impressed.

"What a pity Lesley's so useless at cross-country and showjumping," said Mrs Rooke as her daughter came to a final halt. "Dressage alone doesn't get you anywhere."

"Oh I don't know about that. There's Olympic dressage, plenty of riding club dressage and even a pony club inter-branch dressage. Perhaps we'll have her representing the Woodbury at Stoneleigh next year." David laughed; he seemed rather pleased at the prospect. "Now, Alice, keep calm, sit very light in the sitting trot and if he tries to get his head up, keep squeezing that inside rein."

Alice nodded. She felt nervous, but no longer weak. She made Saffron overbend a little as she walked round the outside, then she tried leg yielding. He was giving his back, relaxing his jaw. The judge tooted at her. Slowly, she thought, very, very slowly, there's tons of time.

166

He was on the bit when she entered at A, but she lost him a little as he came to a halt, she squeezed the rein and put him back on the bit before she saluted. As she trotted round she could feel Saffron gradually settling down and relaxing. He seemed to recognise the familiar markers and to begin to feel at home. By the time she turned him into the serpentine he was going well and she was able to concentrate on making the right-sized loops.

Then they cantered, and she was so pleased with him for staying on the bit that she nearly told him what a clever pony he was, but choked the words back just in time. The circle seemed all right but her transition down to trot went wrong, his back went stiff, his head began to go up and she had risen at the the the trot when she should have been sitting. But he relaxed when they were walking and she was able to keep him on the bit as they began trotting again, and now he was going round to his best side and everything became easier. At last she was turning down the centre. G seemed very close to the judge, this time she looked at her and smiled when she saluted.

"You clever boy," she told Saffron as she rode out and was allowed to speak again. The Woodbury people rushed up to pat him. "Well done," they said, "he didn't stargaze at all."

Lesley gave her a small smile. "David said you were doing well. Now we've got to keep our fingers crossed for Lizzie, because Harry's going to make a complete mess of it, he's practically in hysterics. David's trying to talk some sense into him."

Alice led Saffron across the collecting ring. David was leaning on his shooting stick and saying, "I don't give a damn what sort of cricket score you knock up. Lizzie will do a reasonable test so you don't matter, but you're going in, and that's an order."

"It's not so bad once you've started," Alice told Hanif, "and by the end I was quite enjoying myself, honestly."

"Just keep your head and stop fussing about scores," added David. "Will you ride round with him, Alice? I want to watch Lizzie."

"Now *he's* furious with me," moaned Hanif as Alice mounted and David limped away.

"No he isn't," said Alice as they walked off, side by side. "Don't you remember when he was furious with Mrs Blacker, he went pale with hard steely eyes and set lips, he's not a bit like that now. Anyway, Sarah panicked before she went in and Paul forgot his test. I expect you get used to this sort of thing if you're a team trainer. Do you want to give Jupe a trot?"

Except for looking down, Lizzie was doing well. She was being very accurate and Rajah was moving with plenty of impulsion and remaining steadily on the bit. His long plodding stride was more cadenced that Ferdinand's but lacked the lightness of Stardust's.

"He goes like a German horse and Stardust more like a French horse," observed David to no one in particular. "Both good in their way."

"Well done, Lizzie," he said as she came out. "I'm going to buy you a collar with upward pointing spikes on it before your next test, but, apart from looking down, you rode that really well."

Alice rode right up to the entrance with Hanif. "Good luck," she said. "It'll soon be over. Lovely cross-country this afternoon."

"Lizzie's done well so you can regard it as a school," said David. "Try and keep him calm, never mind about doing the movements at markers."

As Hanif rode round, Mr Franklin appeared with an expensive-looking camera. "I must keep out of sight," he told Lizzie and Alice. "Can I hide between your ponies?"

The judge tooted her car horn and, to all the Woodbury supporters' horror, Jupiter immediately broke into a sideways canter and bounced his way towards A. But Harry suddenly decided not to enter, he turned the pony and rode him all the way round outside the arena on the other rein. Gradually they settled into a trot, and this time, when they reached A, they entered. Jupiter *was* trotting, but he was bounding along far too full of life and not under control at all. It was obvious that Hanif was going to have a battle on his hands if he tried to halt at X. He didn't try, he went on, slowing down gently and halted at G. He took off his cap, but Jupiter was impatient to be off so the cap went on again very quickly, and they bustled on. The serpentine was performed at a very brisk pace and then Jupiter bounced eagerly into a canter and circled far too fast. However, to the anxious watchers' great surprise, he consented to come back to a trot and then a walk as he changed the rein. Going round the other way, Hanif eased him into a very gentle trot and managed his second serpentine at a much more controlled pace. The second canter and circle were better too and finally he trotted down the centre and halted quite obediently at G.

"One huge sigh of relief all round," said David. "And it's a good sign if you finish going better than you started. He's not an easy pony, but I think we're making an impression."

"You certainly are," agreed Mr Franklin, emerging from his hiding place. "A couple of weeks ago he would have left the arena at full gallop and disappeared into the carpark. I'll just get a photograph as they come out."

Hanif was patting Jupiter and looking at David, trying to tell from his expression whether he had done well enough.

"Yes, you did all right," David told him. "You used your legs and your brains. No instructor can ask for more. We'll get the old horse sorted out in the end. These things take time."

"If everyone's finished, can we have lunch?" asked Rupert.

"Yes, small drinks and feeds for ponies and riders taking part in the cross-country." David looked at his watch. "There's an hour and a half to digest."

"We've lost Tina," said Lizzie, looking round with a worried expression.

"No, it's just that the individuals are doing each section in a bunch at the end, but Julia and Oliver are looking after her. As soon as you've eaten we'll walk the cross-country," David went on. "Or at least you will. Mr Franklin's going to drive me from fence to fence."

169

Lynne and Lesley were the happiest people at lunch as they had both finished for the day and felt that they had done well. Hanif was much more cheerful now that the dressage was over, but Rupert's gloom increased minute by minute. Sarah had seen a plan of the course and said there were two waters and a ditch, as well as a quarry, and they were all bound to have black plastic.

Mr Franklin and Mrs Rooke had got together over the marks and kept rushing to the scoreboard to see if the dressage results were out yet. It seemed that the Frog-morton had won the turnout, and the East Tulworth the quiz, but by very small margins. The Washouts had tied second in the quiz, while The Wonders were a very close third in the turnout, but as their combined marks were good they'd moved up to second place overall, while the Washouts were tying third with several other teams. The Cranford Vale hadn't entered, to everyone's surprise.

"We're nine points ahead of you," Sarah told the Wash-outs, when she had seen her mother's score sheet.

"The whole thing is wide open," Mr Franklin told her firmly. "Nine points is nothing at this stage. We'll have much more idea where we stand once the dressage marks are out, but as David says the final results depend heavily on the cross-country."

"I wish you'd all shut up about the cross-country, it's putting me off my lunch," complained Rupert.

"Now concentrate," said David when they were all assembled at the start. "No chattering about other things. Lynne and Lesley, you'd better come in the car, I don't want you distracting the riders. Mr Roberts is going to walk round with you and make sure that you notice the yellow direction arrows and work out a sensible approach, I'll wait for you at each fence. Now, this is the start. Don't start before you're told. See you at fence number one."

It was a straight run to the first fence, a brush, built out in the middle of a field.

"It's a bit low. Ours will trip over it," James told Hanif in a dissatisfied voice. But everyone else was pleased with it.

170

"Always ride carefully at first fences," David told them. "Your pony may not realise that this is a cross-country course. He may be thinking of his stable companion or his next feed, so make absolutely sure he's concentrating. And, as this fence is stuck out in the middle of a field, make quite sure he doesn't surprise you by running out. O.K.?"

Number two was straight ahead, rustic rails with cross poles, and this was set in an actual fence.

"Nice and easy, none of your ponies should mind that," said David. "But you are still going away from home and stable companions, so ride at it."

In the next field there was a yellow direction arrow.

"Everyone see that?" asked Mr Roberts, "and do you all know that it's there to help you? It doesn't matter which side you go of it, or anything like that. You *must* always jump between the flags on the fences, of course, and leave the red on your right and the white on your left."

"Number three's the quarry," announced Sarah as they obeyed the arrow and turned right. They came to a grassy hollow surrounded by thorn bushes. A low but very stout pole was followed by a slope. The pony club members looked at it doubtfully.

"No problem," said David. "You just pop over. It's exactly what you've been doing on Coppice Hill for the last week. Come up slowly, or half-halt if you can, pop over and start looking for the next fence."

A yellow arrow pointed into a thicket of thorn bushes and the pony club members ran down to look. A large tree trunk, on a bend in the path, was hidden by thorn bushes until you were almost upon it.

"It's a good jump," said David when he caught up with them. "A test of impulsion. You all ought to do it all right. Come round the bend slowly but with plenty of energy, make sure your pony knows there's something exciting ahead. Now go back to number three and make sure you know where to look for four as you jump it."

Number five was a rustic gate built into the next fence, and then they had to swing right-handed towards a spinney.

171

"Don't cut the corner," said Mr Roberts as they approached. "Always walk the way you mean to ride. If you head for the direction arrow and *then* turn, that'll bring you in to the fence at a good angle."

David was waiting by the post and rails into the narrow wood.

"The fence is easy," he told them, "but ponies don't like jumping into woods. They don't like jumping into the dark, so you'll have to ride twice as hard as usual. This spinney's not particularly dark as there aren't many leaves on the trees yet, but don't take chances."

Another post and rails took them into a ploughed field and a direction arrow sent them left, along the headland beside the spinney.

"Keep on the headland," said Mr Roberts. "The plough's very holding and will tire the ponies."

The spinney ended at a brook and there was a ford with a gravelled bottom to cross.

"It's not nearly as wide as the Vole," remarked Lizzie cheerfully. "I don't think Ra will mind that."

"It's numbered eight." David, who had crossed by a narrow plank bridge, pointed out from the other side, "So it counts as a fence and dithering on the brink will go down as a refusal."

On the far side of the brook, number nine was a bank with a pole on top.

"No problem as long as you have plenty of impulsion and look where you're going," said David. "People looking down into the ford could have a stop, Lizzie please note, and it could be difficult for the little ponies if they've run out of steam."

Mr Franklin had had to leave the car on the other side of the brook and he fussed round David who insisted on limping all the way to number ten. It was a grid, and the pony club members, who had gone on ahead, didn't like it very much.

"They're jolly short distances for a big one like Ferdie," complained James, pacing them out.

"It's a double bounce, isn't it? Just land and take off," observed Paul.

"It's where Rosie falls flat on her nose. She's never done three jumps in a row before," said Rupert gloomily.

"At least they're good solid telegraph poles and wired to these great lumps of tree trunk: they're not going to break or fall down," announced Hanif approvingly.

"The secret of success is to look at the last one," said David, hobbling up. "Look at it and ride for it. Ignore the other two. If you do run out you have to re-take them all—it's numbered as one jump, you see. But you won't have any trouble if you come at a slow canter with plenty of impulsion, a feel on both reins, and look at the last one."

After the grid, the course turned left-handed and they were on their way home. Number eleven was a steep, muddy slide down to the brook, which they then had to wade across, before jumping out over a tree trunk on the far bank, which was numbered twelve.

The pony club members looked down the slide despondently.

"Ugh, the ponies aren't going to like that."

"Ra will be horrified."

"The slide's nothing," said David firmly, "but don't let them dither because it counts as a fence. The problem is how to explain to the ponies that you don't expect them to jump the brook *and* the tree trunk all in one. If you ride straight at the water they'll think that's what you want, and as it's too wide for them they'll refuse. So you go down the slide, *slant* them at the water. Make it quite clear you're not interested in getting across, then, when you're *in* the water, show them the jump on the far side. Do you understand what I'm getting at? It's important, because this is where a misunderstanding between horse and rider could arise."

The pony club members made their plans and then went on to fence thirteen while Mr Franklin and Mr Roberts helped David over an even narrower plank bridge and back to the car.

Thirteen was a ditch with a pole above. It was quite a

deep ditch and by the time David reached them the pony club members were all gazing into the bottom of it with fearful faces.

"Rule number one," said David. "Never look into the bottom of a ditch. It's the width that matters, not the depth."

"We'll never jump that."

"Of course you will. We've been practising for this."

"Our ditch was brown and shallow, not deep and green with water in the bottom."

"It's on the way home and with the pole over the top the ponies will take off the right distance away. They won't even know there's a ditch there, unless you're all shaking and quaking so much they begin to think there's something wrong. Just ride at the pole, look up, and throw your hearts over."

Lynne began to say that she was glad she hadn't got to ride round such an awful course, but her father told her to keep quiet.

"I like it," announced Alice. "Well, so far."

"I don't like that grid much, nor the second river jump," said James. "They're a bit trappy for Ferdie. He likes the sort of course where you can gallop on a bit."

"So does Jupe, but *I* like a bit of trappiness to slow him down."

"Your wish is granted," Alice told Hanif as they came to the lambing pen. "You couldn't have anything much more trappy than that."

James groaned. "This is the end."

The pen was an oblong, built of straw bales, with a wattle jump in at one end and then a sharp right turn out over more wattles.

"You can see the problem," said David. "The larger ponies and the tearaways will jump in and then go straight on over the straw bales and be eliminated for taking the wrong course. You've got to slow right down to nothing, pop in, reins, legs, weight and eyes all turning him to the right as you land. If you jump in on the left it'll give you a bit more room. Small ponies are a bit suspicious **of pens and** inclined to stop. You drive on hard. Harry, you're the most likely to come to grief here."

"I'll creep and pop," promised Hanif, pacing out the distance.

The last fence was a length of dry stone wall which had been built into the field fence.

"No problem," said David, "unless anyone has a very tired pony. Now you go for the finish. Between those two flags over there. If you forget it you'll be eliminated, so, when you land over the last, don't think, 'hurrah, I've done it'. Think 'finish!'"

"Finish, finish," said Paul, pushing Sarah.

"Rupert, are you listening?" asked Netti.

"What?" he asked.

"The finish!" they all shouted at him. "You *must* go through it. You'll be elminiated if you don't."

"Look, over there." They marched him towards the flags.

David was waiting for them at the finish. "The bigger ponies will have no trouble about getting round in the time, but the little ones will have to keep going. They can't afford refusals, as they'll be clocking up time faults. You're allowed three refusals at each fence, as it's a novice event. If you lose count consult the jump judges. And be polite to them and all stewards. You can be eliminated for rudeness to officials, and the fact that you're excited or upset is no defence. The supporters must *not* shout advice or instructions to the riders as that can get them eliminated too. It's an easy course to find your way round, so you shouldn't get lost, but don't forget the finish."

David looked at his watch. "They're due to start in ten minutes, so we'd better get tacked up and think about a practice jump."

They met Tina and Oliver in the horsebox park. Tina said that her turnout marks were awful—the worst in the Woodbury—her quiz questions had been lovely, except for one, and Hobbit had gone on the wrong leg in the dressage.

175

David drove over to give Julia some advice about things she was to be sure to tell Tina as they walked the cross-country, then he stationed himself beside the practice jump, a rustic pole on oil drums and waited for the Woodbury riders who were pulling on their polo-neck sweaters and then tying on each other's huge back and front numbers.

Jupiter was so delighted to see a jump at last that he flung himself over as though it was a four-foot triple, but Hanif found that he didn't mind that sort of behaviour any more. He just laughed and took him round again, until after three jumps and a good deal of cantering about, Jupiter settled down.

Rosie, in a vague mood, looking around her and at the other ponies, forgot to take off and, tripping over the jump, nearly landed on her nose, but, as Rupert said, this seemed to do her good, as she then jumped much more carefully than usual.

Alice, pleased to have her martingale on again, was feeling quite cheerful about everything but the lambing pen. She kept rehearsing how she would jump it in her mind, but with Saffron feeling so calm and confident beneath her, she couldn't be too worried.

Lizzie was anxious, so much seemed to depend on her doing a good round, and David kept roaring at her to look up.

"Except for the first two and the last they're all fences where looking ahead is *essential*," he told her.

"I really will try terribly hard," promised Lizzie.

The Wonders, on their more seasoned ponies, didn't have to do so much warming up, and when they had all had a couple of practise jumps, Berry and Stardust were left in the charge of the horsebox driver and the whole Woodbury part moved up to the collecting ring.

The scene had changed. There were spectators and jump judges beside the fences, more spectators and mounted runners hurrying about in between.

Lesley and Lynne, who had stayed to watch the early competitors, came running to meet their teams. "The

176

Brackenhurst did very well, they had three clears, and the first two from the South Barset went well, but the one's who's coming in now has had masses of refusals and the last one to go has been ages in the quarry."

"Shush," said Lizzie, "You mustn't sound so *pleased*."

"Why on earth not?" snapped Lesley.

"Because we don't want people being pleased when we fall in the water," answered Rupert.

David had Mrs Morgan and Mr Roberts checking girths. Mrs Roberts was handing out barley sugar to non-riders. James had gone to the start, Netti circled, waiting for her call. The last of the South Barsets had fallen off at the grid. There was a delay until the pony was caught.

At last Ferdinand was on his way. He started fast and made the first two fences look easy, then he vanished down the slope into the quarry. He reappeared, heading for the rustic gate, jumped that and disappeared again into the spinney.

Mr Franklin had produced a pair of binoculars and, standing on the seat of his car with the roof open, was trying to give a running commentary.

"Ah, here he is, out of the ford and up the bank. He's steadied for the grid, one, two, three." But then Netti started, and with two of them on the course, no one knew where to look. Sarah was called to the start. David told Paul not to canter Banjo round and round, he had more than enough work ahead of him. Mr Franklin announced that James was through the lambing pen and Netti just coming up the bank.

Lizzie and Rupert were walking round together, reciting, "Look up!" and, "Finish!" to each other.

James galloped through the finish and then rode over to David, his solemn face suddenly transformed by a huge smile.

"It was great," he said breathlessly as he patted Ferdinand. "I didn't have any trouble that I know of. He was brilliant over the streams and that pen thing. I don't think he even noticed the ditch."

"Well done, you looked very good from here," David told him.

"How's Netti doing?" asked James as his mother rushed up with a handful of pony nuts.

"Terribly well, but Sarah's being rather slow. Get off, darling, and loosen his girths."

"Netti's over the pen, but Sarah's stopped at the spinney. Ah, it's all right, she's over this time," announced Mr Franklin.

Paul was looking grim, he *had* to be clear.

"Don't go mad, you can't do more than you can," David told him.

Netti came galloping in. "Oh, he was brilliant!" she shrieked, dismounting and patting Tristram excitedly. "He was really brilliant and I enjoyed every minute. The jumps are lovely, Lizzie, Rupert, I promise you. The jumps are really gorgeous."

Mr Franklin was making disapproving noises. "Silly girl, she's turned round on top of the slide, but Paul's going very well. That little black of his has a surprising turn of speed."

The starter was calling Hanif.

"Keep calm, you've a few minutes' wait yet," David told him. "Sarah's taking her time and Paul's not going to keep that speed up for long."

As Sarah rode in, Hanif started out. He let Jupiter gallop on over the first two fences and then slowed him right down for the quarry. Mr Franklin took his eyes off his stepson for a moment and announced that Paul was safely over the grid, then he went back to Hanif. "Harry's going great guns," he told David. "I hope the pony's not running away. No, he's steadied him for the spinney, he's in. And Paul's over the ditch, coming up to the lambing pen, but the pony's slowed down a lot. Oh dear, he's stopped." A groan went up from the Wonders.

"Harry's over the grid," shouted Mr Franklin excitedly, "and Paul's got going again."

David had sent Mr Robert's to pull up Alice's girths.

"Get them up another hole if you can. That's the sort of pony which loses weight on a long gallop."

Paul came in slowly, he seemed very cast down. "He just couldn't go any faster. I suppose I'll have time faults as well as a refusal."

"Jump off, loosen his girths and turn his head to the wind," said David, looking at the blowing pony. "He went as fast as he could."

Mrs Roberts arrived with barley sugar and a handful of oats.

"Harry's managed to slow down for the lambing pen, he's gone to the left and he's trotting. He's done it," shouted Mr Franklin, sounding like a radio commentator who's just seen a vital goal scored in the World Cup. "He's only got to do the wall and he's home."

No one heard how Alice was doing because Mr Franklin left his post and rushed to the finish to welcome Hanif home, but she was enjoying herself. She loved the feeling of galloping over the grass, looking for the next fence. There seemed to be lots of time and plenty of space between them. She felt clear-headed and happy. Saffron felt happy too. A pop, he seemed to agree, when he saw the way into the quarry. Now where? He followed her gaze.

He didn't mind the spinney; the ford he took as a matter of course, the grid carefully and neatly. The slide and the brook he summed up quickly. I know how to do that, he told her. He didn't notice the ditch. He let her slow him right down for the pen, he popped in and then, realising what was wanted, turned and jumped out. They galloped for the stone wall and the finish.

Mr Franklin, suddenly remembering Hanif's team mates, rushed back to watch. He was in time to announce that Lizzie, who had started well, had stopped at the spinney, but was over at the second attempt and that Alice was finishing very fast indeed.

"Good luck and don't forget the finish," David told Rupert as he took a suspicious glance at his girths.

"Lizzie's done the grid," shouted Mr Franklin.

179

"Any trouble, Alice?" asked David, as Rupert set off towards the first fence.

"No, it was lovely. He jumped every one perfectly." She gave Saffron a handful of pony nuts.

"Lizzie's over the second brook, heading for the ditch," reported Mr Franklin.

"How's Rupert doing?" asked Hanif. "Lizzie had a stop," he told Alice.

"I've lost him, he must still be in the quarry," answered Mr Franklin. "No, there he is. He's over the rustic gate. He's cut the corner a bit. He's giving her a very short run, but he's done it."

"I don't suppose we'll ever see him again. Knowing Rupert, he'll forget to turn left," said Lesley.

"Lizzie's crawling up to the pen. She's in, and she's out. Now she's really galloping."

"We can see her. Tell us how Rupert's doing."

"He's over the brook, approaching the grid."

"Rosie'll never do it," said Netti, standing in her stirrups and trying to see.

"She's having a try," reported Mr Franklin. "Heavens! Something went wrong over the last one, she practically stood on her head. How that boy stayed on . . ."

"He always does. His legs are so long and so aptly constructed," Netti chanted triumphantly.

"Touch wood," shrieked Lynne.

Lizzie came galloping in as Rupert disappeared down the slide, and the first of the Frogmorton team started.

"Oh, that was fantastic!" said Lizzie, dismounting. "I never thought he'd go so well, but I'm afraid I've let the Washouts down though, because I did have one stop. He insisted on a good look before he would jump into the spinney."

"You did very well," David told her. "*I* didn't expect a clear round from old Safety First at his first outing."

"Rupert's doing brilliantly so far," Netti told her sister.

"He's over the ditch, no trouble there. He's going pretty fast. I hope he remembers to slow up for the pen. Too fast, he's in, but he's not going to turn, he's going straight on.

180

No, he's refused. Well, he's collided with the straw bales. He's turned and he's out," shouted Mr Franklin.

The pony club members were all climbing back on their ponies to see Rupert finish.

"Isn't Rosie going fast."

"I didn't know she could gallop like that."

"Good old Rupert," shouted Oliver as his brother jumped the last.

"Will him to go through the finish," shrieked Netti.

Rosie went through the flags so fast that it was some way before Rupert could pull up, then he dismounted and led her back, looking round vaguely for David.

"That was terrific," he said, "I did just about everything wrong, but it was still terrific. I wish we could come back tomorrow and have another go."

"Did you have any refusals?" asked Lesley impatiently.

"Dozens, I should think. I got lost in the quarry. We hit the last pole of the grid a fearful clonk, but I think it stayed up. Then we went down the slide too fast and practically fell in the river. We took that pen thing too fast as well and she refused the straw bales, which was a bit of luck really as we weren't meant to jump them. While she was stationary I managed to haul her round and point her at the wattles and she was terribly pleased to see an easy way out. Poor old Rosie," he went on, patting her, "I'm afraid you had a lot of frights."

"But how many refusals did you have?" asked Lesley in an exasperated voice.

"Did you circle or turn round in the quarry?" asked Lizzie.

"I don't think so, I just got lost and wandered about in the bushes. And in the pen we sort of collided with the bales, I don't think I turned round."

"You'll have to wait and see what the judges say," David told Lesley. "He didn't have any time faults. You did well," he told Rupert, "and Rosie's got the makings of a good cross-country pony. She needs experience and a bit more education. Now you'd better all water and feed while we're waiting for the results."

"Hold it," said Oliver. "Julia sent me to tell you that one of the Froggie ponies isn't going. It's gone lame, so she's persuaded the collecting steward to put Tina in the space. They went dashing off for a practice jump, but they're back now."

"Oh we must stay and watch Hobby," said Lizzie.

"I think Tina's going to mess things up," Oliver sounded gloomy. "Her teeth keep chattering and she's gone pale grey with fright."

"I'll go and see if I can cheer her up," said David, limping off towards the start.

The pony club members turned their attention back to the course. The Frogmorton team had taken off their black jackets and donned polo-necks like everyone else, but their elegant little ponies didn't seem at home on the cross-country. The first one had gone so slowly that the second one caught up with it and they came through the finish together. Then the third one set off and Tina took her place at the start. Julia checked her girths. David said, "Take it steady. Just try to get round."

Tina could only nod miserably, as she tried to control her chattering teeth.

"You'll be all right once you get going," David told her. "I can remember feeling ghastly before my first race."

Tina set off with fumbling hands and weak legs, her mind was taken up with how awful she felt. Hobbit knew his stable companions were all in the collecting ring, *he* didn't want to leave them and go out in to the unknown, and sensing that his rider also disliked the expedition, he went slowly and without his usual zest. He came to a stop at the first fence.

"I knew it," groaned Oliver.

"Oh go on, Tina, don't be feeble," said Sarah.

"Legs!" added Alice.

Tina suddenly woke up to the horror of her situation. She might not even get over the first fence. Ollie would never forgive her. She shook herself into action and gave the surprised Hobbit a whack.

"Short run and legs," she told herself. Hobbit, finding that she did want to go after all, decided to oblige. He jumped the brush and cantered on towards the crossed rails. By the time they reached the quarry Tina had forgotten herself and was concentrating on the course. Flying in and out of the spinney, a sensation of pleasure began to creep over pony and rider. Hobbit forded the brook willingly, jumped the grid neatly and then they caught up with the third Frogmorton pony, dithering with horror at the top of the slide.

"Clear the course," shouted the jump judge. "Stand to the side, number thirty-four. Let the next pony through."

"Get out of the way and I'll give you a lead," shouted Tina. Hobbit slid down carefully, splashed through the brook, jumped the pole and galloped for the ditch.

Oliver gave cries of triumph as Hobbit reappeared, leading the Frogmorton pony home.

"She's clocked up a few time faults, I'm afraid," said David, looking at his watch. "But they may let her off some of them if the other pony held her up."

The Wheelers all rushed to congratulate Hobbit, and a few minutes later the mothers began to emerge from the course.

"I've been watching by that horrible slide." Mrs Franklin was wearing green jeans and short yellow gumboots instead of her usual sari. "I am very proud of you, Hanif. You have done so well. Both our teams are doing very well."

Mrs Wheeler was looking at her children with new eyes. "I never knew that you were all so accomplished," she said. "You've been telling me for years that Rupert was the most hopeless tack-cleaner on earth, yet he's got seventy-five marks for turnout. You told me that Rosie and Ra couldn't jump and then I find you flying round the most terrifying-looking course."

Mrs Spencer had rushed to hug Tina. "You were great," she told her. "I nearly died when you refused the first one, but after that you got going and you were fantastic. The way you yelled at the little Frogmorton girl on top of that terrifying slide. Oh, Tina," she hugged her again, "I never realised that when I joined you to the pony club it would lead to this."

"No," agreed Tina, who was rather embarrassed by all the hugging, "and it wouldn't have come to this if Ollie hadn't lent me Hobbit."

"You must be proud of your elder daughter," Mr Franklin told Mrs Rooke as they hurried back to the collecting ring area, carrying the latest scores, "To come out top in the dressage, that really is something."

"Oh yes, well, Lesley's a specialist by nature, but Sarah has a more balanced character. She's a real all-rounder. I expect you noticed that not many of the younger children took part in all four events."

Lesley's won the dressage!" Hanif shouted the good news as his stepfather handed a carefully-marked score sheet to David, who had been sat down in the car and was being given coffee by Mrs Roberts.

"Well done, Lesley."

"David said you were good."

"Will she get a rosette?"

Then, to Alice's amazement, her Aunt Margaret appeared.

"You have done well," she said, smiling her thin smile. "I had no idea you could do dressage and cross-country."

"I had no idea you were coming," answered Alice.

"Well, it hadn't occured to me, but then Clare suddenly arrived. She's home from Turkey. I think she's finished with her latest boyfriend, and she wanted to come. She said it would remind her of *her* pony club days—not that she ever attempted a dressage test. Ah, here she comes. She stopped to get your score."

"Hullo, Alice. Your lot are doing terribly well. You've acquired eight hundred and thirty five marks without counting the cross-country," said Clare, who had Uncle Peter's rather square figure, Aunt Margaret's decided manner, combined with a much more cheerful expression. "You're lying second and the other Woodbury team are only ten behind you. And doesn't Sandra Crankshaw's

Saffy look *different?* He used to have a dreadful skinny neck and charge about with his ears in Sandra's face. I can't imagine how you've persuaded him to do dressage."

All the other Woodbury members were pressed round David.

"How are we doing?"

"Did Lesley really win the dressage?"

"Yes, with a hundred and eighteen points. Three ahead of her nearest rival. But the rest of you haven't done too badly. James and Netti—a hundred and six. Lizzie, a hundred and four. Alice, a hundred and three. Harry, ninety-eight. Well, you can all see for yourselves in a moment."

"But how are we doing in the whole competition?" asked James impatiently.

"It all depends on the cross-country. There are six teams more or less level-pegging at the moment. It looks to me as though the one with three clear rounds will win."

"But both our teams are in the first six," added Mr Franklin proudly. "And the other six are right out of it."

"Go and put the ponies away," said David when they had all had a look at the score sheet. "It's bound to take some time to sort out the cross-country scores and do the final adding up."

The ponies knew they had done well. They accepted their owners praise and cossetting graciously, feeling that it was theirs by right. Ferdinand and Jupiter looked very superior in their dark blue, fishnet sweat rugs. The cattle truck ponies were all wearing rugs of some sort. Lesley was bandaging Stardust's legs. Alice had no rug, but she brushed out Saffron's saddle mark and gave him an enormous feed. She was feeling desperately sad. She knew this was really the end of the holidays. The course was over, soon she'd start school. Saffron would be sent back. Supposing Mr Crankshaw sold him? She loved him so much, she thought, swallowing tears. She'd never love another pony so much, even if they could find one to hire next holidays. Hanif was calling her, his mother had made

185

far too much tea. He pleaded with her to come and help him eat it. She went over, trying to force a cheerful smile on her face.

They were still eating when Oliver came running. "David says there are rosettes to six places so he thinks both teams will get them. You're all to come up looking tidy, wearing jackets and crash caps," he told them.

"I needn't bother, need I?" asked Tina, who had already put her borrowed jacket in Mrs Rooke's car.

"He said 'everyone'," answered Oliver, "so I expect you'd better."

They all walked up together.

"If only we'd had one of the Washouts in our team, we'd have had a really good chance of winning," complained James, who had borrowed his mother's score sheet and studied everybody's marks. "If we'd had you, Alice, we'd certainly have won, and with Lesley too, we'd have been streets ahead of all the other teams."

"But it wouldn't have been so much fun, because the rest of us would have been nowhere," Lizzie pointed out.

Mrs Rooke bustled round inspecting them. "Rupert, your shirt's out, your tie's crooked and you can't wear your cap on the back of your head like that," she snapped. "Paul, there's orange juice on your face. Do up your jacket buttons, Alice."

David was sitting in the Franklin's car, and, as they gathered round, he asked, "Do the boys all know they have to take off their crash caps if they're given rosettes? The girls only have to say thank you and smile."

"Rupert, did you hear," demanded Netti. "You take your cap off."

Oliver rushed up. "They've taken down the scoreboard and they're adding the cross-country marks," he announced, and rushed away again.

A moment later he reappeared, waving his arms excitedly. "They've given Rupert a clear. You've six hundred cross-country points."

The Washouts looked at each other and hope grew.

186

"Great!"

"Fantastic!"

"That means you didn't turn your back, then." Lesley looked at Rupert accusingly.

"It means they've beaten us," moaned Sarah.

"We knew that. We both had two clears and one dodgy round, but they were already fifteen points ahead." No one listened to James.

Lynne, Paul and Sarah raced after Oliver. David had climbed out of the car and the others walked beside him as he headed slowly towards the table that had been set up for the rosettes.

Mrs Franklin appeared with a picnic chair. "Will you sit down, please," she said, offering it to David.

"No, I'm all right. I've been sitting in the car." David waved her away.

"Persuade him to sit, Hanif. He must, he is exhausted."

Hanif opened the chair. "It's no good, David. She's a terrible bully. You'd better surrender with dignity because she'll win in the end."

"Put it round to the side then," said David with a sigh. "I don't want to sit bang in the middle, looking like a presiding judge."

With David sitting, most of the Woodbury members collapsed on the ground around him and tried to wait patiently for the final results. They didn't have to wait long. Suddenly Mr Franklin and Mrs Rooke detached themselves from the crowd round the scoreboard and hurried over. Mr Franklin was trying hard not to look too pleased.

"First and third," he told David quietly. "They've labelled your lot Woodbury A," he added, turning to Hanif, "so don't be thrown into confusion when they call you."

The Washouts gave no shout of triumph, partly because they didn't quite believe they had won, and partly because they didn't want to crow over the defeated Wonders.

Then Oliver rushed over and broke the tension by shouting, "Tina's sixth in the Junior Individual. You are," he repeated, seeing the blank look on Tina's face. "You're sixth *and* you get a rosette, I asked the secretary."

"Oh Ollie, you shouldn't bother officials..." Lizzie began but they shushed her as the Area Representative began to speak.

"She was a famous showjumper when she was young," Paul told the others. "I've got a photograph of her in one of my books."

She was telling them what they already knew, that the Area Cup was a new idea especially to encourage pony clubs which couldn't produce teams of the standard required for the main interbranch events, and to bring on the younger members. Then she thanked the organizers, congratulated them on their efficiency, and came at last to the winning teams.

"First, Woodbury A. Second, East Tulworth. Third, Woodbury B. Fourth, Brackenhurst. Fifth, South Barset. Sixth, Northdown."

Walking forward in a row, the five Washouts *had* to believe that they had won. This was no dream.

"Congratulations," said Jill Donaldson five times as she handed them their red rosettes and, "Many Congratulations," as she held out the large silver cup. "You must all be very proud that The Woodbury will be the first name on it."

Lesley and Lizzie took the cup, the boys' hands were too full of crash caps and rosettes to carry any more. Everyone clapped and the photographer told them to hold it high. Then, as the East Tulworth were called in, they rushed out and Lizzie handed it straight to David.

"You really won it," she said. "None of us would have come anywhere at all without you."

David looked from the cup to Lizzie and then smiled. "Well, let's say it was a combined effort," he suggested. "I couldn't have done it without five people prepared to put up with my roars of rage and really work. Here, come on, clap the Wonders, all of you, I can't."

James and Netti came back carrying their yellow rosettes and trying to stifle feelings of disappointment and envy, but

Lynne and Paul, who were truly delighted, rushed to show theirs to their parents. Sarah gave hers a look of disgust and stuffed it in her pocket.

The senior individuals had been given their rosettes. The juniors were called forward and Tina took her place at the end of the line. She came back smiling. "The first thing I've ever won, but it's yours, Ollie. They go with the pony."

Oliver looked at the rosette in horror. "Why did it have to be pink? Ugh, it's a colour I can't stand. You keep it, Tina. I'll wait until next year and try to win one myself."

The Area Representative was explaining that so many people had tied first in the quiz, turnout and cross-country sections that it was impossible to award special rosettes, but in the dressage two riders had been outstanding: Lesley Rooke of the Woodbury and Amanda Goddard of the East Tulworth, and would they come forward for their rosettes.

Everyone but Sarah clapped enthusiastically, and Netti and Lynne shocked by this unsisterly attitude, each took one of Sarah's hands and clapped them for her.

Lesley came back looking rather dazed, and took the large red and white rosette with *Special* across the centre to show David.

Mrs Rooke swept up bossily. "You look all in, David. I've sent Mr Franklin to fetch my car and I'll take you home at once."

"Oh, I'm O.K.," said David, struggling to his feet. "I've enjoyed it and there's nothing like a little success to drive away the aches and pains. Well done, all of you," he told the pony club members. "I'm very pleased with the way you all went." He looked round at their faces, "Don't you think, Mrs Rooke, that there's something about our pony club? They look much nicer than anyone else's."

"They performed better today, and that's what counts," snapped Mrs Rooke opening the car door.

Alice's relations reappeared. "Congratulations Alice. We're bursting with pride," said Clare. "If only I'd done something like this in my pony club days, but teams and cups and red rosettes seemed an unattainable dream. I've

189

been telling Mum that she must get a move on and arrange to buy Saffy from old Crankshaw. I imagine he's what you want most in the world?"

"Oh yes, the only thing really. But it's difficult about money," explained Alice sadly.

"The Trustees have to wait until probate is granted . . .," Aunt Margaret began in her dreary voice, which almost welcomed the fact that nothing could be done.

"Oh, don't be dotty, Mum. You and Dad could easily lend Alice the money until that happens and, if you don't do something quickly the Crankshaws will hear how much Saffy's improved and ask twice as much," said Clare, who had learned how to manage her mother. "You'd be mad not to fix the whole thing up tonight."

"I'll discuss it with Daddy."

Hearing the unenthusiastic note in her Aunt's voice, Alice's fragile hopes collapsed, but then her cousin smiled at her. "Don't worry, we'll persuade them somehow," whispered Clare.

"Hold it everyone." Mr Franklin had produced a large bottle of cider and was pouring it into the cup. "Before we go home we must all drink to the future of the Woodbury Pony Club. You take the cup round, Harry, David first."

"To the Woodbury, remembering that a pony club is only as good as its members," said David and drank.

"But that's not true," objected James, "except for Alice and Harry and Tina, we've all been members for years and it's always been a pathetic pony club, really boring and hopeless; everyone said so."

"Right," agreed Rupert. "I'll drink to the new and transformed Woodbury," he grabbed the cup and drank greedily.

"If only the Cranford Vale had been here to see," moaned Netti, "you know how they despise us, they'll go round telling everyone that the standard must have been absolutely ghastly if the Woodbury won."

"Drink," ordered Hanif, offering her the cup. "And stop *worrying*. Now we've got David to teach us we're all going to become fantastically good riders and amaze the world."

'JINNY' BOOKS

by Patricia Leitch

When Jinny Manders rescues Shantih, a chestnut Arab, from a cruel circus, her dreams of owning a horse of her own seem to come true. But Shantih is wild and unrideable.

This is an exciting and moving series of books about a very special relationship between a girl and a magnificent horse.

FOR LOVE OF A HORSE
A DEVIL TO RIDE
THE SUMMER RIDERS
NIGHT OF THE RED HORSE
GALLOP TO THE HILLS
HORSE IN A MILLION
THE MAGIC PONY
RIDE LIKE THE WIND
CHESTNUT GOLD
JUMP FOR THE MOON

Armada

Here are some of the most recent titles in our exciting fiction series:

☐ Journey to Atlantis *J. J. Fortune* £1.75
☐ The Feud in the Chalet School
   Elinor M. Brent-Dyer £1.75
☐ Tomb of Nightmares *J. H. Brennan* £1.95
☐ The Emerald-Eyed Cat Mystery *Carolyn Keene* £1.75
☐ The Demon's Den *Franklin W. Dixon* £1.75
☐ The Mystery of the Kidnapped Whale
   Marc Brandel £1.75
☐ Horse of Fire *Patricia Leitch* £1.75
☐ The Garden of Madness *David Tant* 1.95

Armadas are available in bookshops and newsagents, but can also be ordered by post.

HOW TO ORDER
ARMADA BOOKS, Cash Sales Dept., GPO Box 29, Douglas, Isle of Man, British Isles. Please send purchase price plus 15p per book (maximum postal charge £3.00). Customers outside the UK also send purchase price plus 15p per book. Cheque, postal or money order — no currency.

NAME (Block letters) _____

ADDRESS _____

_____

_____